Mol

Diane Chesterton

This is a work of fiction. Names, characters, places, and incidents either are the product of the author's imagination or are used fictitiously. Apart from historical figures and events, any resemblance to actual persons, living or dead, events, or locales is entirely coincidental.

First published September 2022

ISBN: 9798354617418

Book design by Diane Chesterton
Jacket Photograph Copyright © 2022 Getty Images
Title Lettering in FairydustB by Marcel de Jong
Author's Name Lettering in Ghost Theory by Fonts Bomb

Dedicated to Sheila.

My guiding light, friend and wonderful Mum.

This book would never have seen the light of day without the encouragement of my Husband and the knowledge of a wonderful Daughter. I am eternally grateful for all you did.

To Philippa Ronan, your friendship and guidance are a treasure beyond words, thank you.

Contents

1645 Onwards

"No! Please stop! I'm not a witch. I did nothing wrong. Let me go!"

Mary struggled and fought against hands she couldn't see. Screaming from within the confines of a burlap sack, the scents of Rye and Ergot remind her how she'd come to be in this situation. She would have laughed if she hadn't been so scared.

She was desperate, but what could she do against strong men? As a slight 16-year-old, she was not equipped to fight them. She pulled away for a minute, but blinded by the sack as she was, she stumbled over roots and fell against the oak tree. Pain shot through her elbow. There was no sympathy from the mob, solid arms yanked her up and held her.

"Please don't do this," she begged as tears ran freely down her face, her stomach tied itself in knots and her body trembled with fear. It didn't make any difference. Her hands were secured tight behind her back. How many men were there? She couldn't be sure, five, ten, twenty? It didn't matter, she was helpless against them. As much as she kicked and fought they didn't stop. She sensed the noose fall loosely around her neck.

"Only one good witch, a dead one. String her up." A man's voice, but Mary didn't know it. A stranger to her, why would he want to hurt her?

Her mind filled with terror. Pulling herself backwards away from where she thought the tree was, she wriggled and twisted trying to get free. This couldn't be happening. James had been her friend, how could he have led her to these men? He betrayed her and stood with his brother while the mob took her.

She screamed as loud as she could, "No! James please. Help me!"

She felt the noose tightening as her feet left the ground. "Oh God! Please help me. Someone, please. I didn't do anyth…"

The noose became too tight to allow speech. She twitched as blood failed to reach her brain. The faint light coming through the sack disappeared as darkness took her. She knew confusion and dizziness, bile filled her mouth. She felt dampness flow down her legs. Then she felt no more.

***

How long she lay at the bottom of the oak tree she didn't know. Her emerald eyes squinted against dappled sunlight. The sack was gone from her head and her elbow didn't hurt anymore. The mob was gone, and for that she was grateful. James and his brother Lawrence were gone too. At the thought of James, tears pricked her eyes, but she gulped them away.

Standing up, she dusted down her bodice and skirt, pushed her dark hair back into its bun and replaced the pins. How she'd survived she didn't know, but all she wanted now was to go home and take solace in her Mother's arms.

She looked back at the oak tree, the hollow where she'd

spent so many happy hours with James, picnicking, playing conkers or just chatting about the world. She wanted to burn it down, but the woods were deep and she didn't want to burn the whole lot down, just the tree. All those happy memories turned sour in one single act. She would never come here again.

Lifting her skirts she ran with ease, heading to the small cottage she shared with her parents, sister and brother. She couldn't believe she'd survived, that the mob had let her live.

Dashing through the open door she called, "Mother where are you?" The cottage was empty. Mary checked upstairs and then headed to the barn. Daisy cow was outside grazing and she stopped to stroke and whisper gently to her. A moo was the response and a nuzzle to her neck.

Mary went back inside the cottage to wait. Where could they have gone? There was always someone here. Alex was only a baby, it wasn't practical to go far with him, Mother or Lizzie should be here looking after him. The fire, banked up, still smouldered red coals so they couldn't have gone too far. She was just considering going outside to call them when she heard voices, children laughing and giggling, and running feet

"Molly stop teasing your Uncle."

Mary moved to the door, that sounded like Lizzie, but who was she talking to? She could see Mother and Lizzie walking up the mud path with two children running towards the cottage. She stared, Mother looked worn, her eyes sad, lines on her face that hadn't been there that morning and Lizzie was ...pregnant?

The children raced into the cottage, "Uncle Alex will you

play conkers with me?" the girl asked.

Mary's mouth dropped open. Uncle Alex? But Alex was just a baby, this boy looked to be 6 or 7 years old.

The children were soon followed indoors by the adults.

"Mother, Lizzie?" Mary said as they passed her without a glance. Mary looked at them aghast, they'd totally disregarded her. What is going on?

Mother went to the kettle, filled it from the water drum and placed it on the fire to boil. "I still can't believe she's gone. Six years and still no answers. Who would do that to Mary? My poor baby girl." Mother's eyes were moist as Lizzie put her arm around her to comfort her.

"The flowers you put on her grave were beautiful, she would have loved them. She's safe with God now, she doesn't suffer. Please, Mother, don't let the children see you so distraught," Lizzie said.

Mary froze to the spot.

Dead!?

She shook her head, "No I'm not dead!"

That couldn't be right. She didn't feel dead. She had thoughts and feelings. Daisy had recognised her. It couldn't be, it just couldn't.

Yet when she looked around she could see the differences. The new cushion on the fireside chair, the high chair for Alex was missing. Small things were changed or moved. She knew it must be true.

It was six years ago?

She was dead.

Her hand trembled first, the tremble rose through her arm to her shoulder and then slowly she started to shake. Her body shook from head to toe. She had gone from the calm of a sunny day to a stormy torrent in a matter of seconds.

"No! No! No!"

She felt herself gasping for breath, but her chest didn't rise or fall.

Her palms were dry, even as she wrung her hands together desperate for a reaction.

She couldn't feel her heart beating as she usually did when she was distressed. Moving trembling fingers to her pulse she checked. Where was her pulse? She checked the other arm, but still no pulse.

It was true.

"It's not fair," she sobbed.

She hadn't done anything wrong.

She had so much more life to live, with all the things a young woman had a right to. She had dreams. Dreams of a loving husband, a sweet child or maybe two, a home and time – lots of time. Those dreams were gone.

Sinking to the floor she banged it with her fists as she cried out… "Noooo!" She stamped her feet and kicked the door nearby, before hitting the floor once more. Tears trickled down her face as the realisation came to her. She had nothing anymore, and would never have anything again. Why would they do this to her? Why was she killed? Why did they accuse her of witchcraft? Then she remembered.

Mr Smith had caused his pregnant wife's death, stealing

Rye contaminated with the fungus Ergot. Ergot causes St. Anthony's Fire, which as everyone knows is deadly. He should have been more careful, but alcohol can have a huge effect on judgement, and the whole village knew he was an alcoholic. He killed his wife then blamed Mary, accused her of witchcraft. All she had done was provide raspberry leaf for tea to help prepare Mrs Smith for the birth of her baby.

That James had helped the mob baffled her. He knew her, he knew she wasn't a witch. She had even thought he might love her, she knew she had been falling in love with him. Why would he lead her to them? And what did his brother have to do with it? Why was he there? Neither of them helped her.

Mr Smith was grief-stricken, so she could sort of understand him wanting to blame her, but James and his brother should have helped her. James' betrayal lay heavy on her heart. She needed to turn her heart to stone or maybe ice. Either way, she couldn't think kindly of him anymore. The careworn look on Mother's face, that was down to James. Some friend he turned out to be. She didn't know how, but she would have revenge on him for this. Somehow, someday she would make him pay.

Dashing the tears from her face she looked at her family.

First, her sister Lizzie, who had grown to be a beautiful (pregnant) woman, then she glanced at the child.

"That must be her daughter, Molly." Mary smiled to herself. Lizzie had always called her Mary-Mol, "did she call her daughter Molly in deference to me?" She was surprised at how pleased that made her. Molly must be three or four she surmised, had to be. "So Lizzie married Ben?" She was glad that the wedding had gone ahead as planned. Although she didn't know for sure it had, Molly had a definite look of Ben about her.

Her brother Alex she noted was growing to be a handsome lad. She couldn't believe how tall he was. A shock of brown hair that could do with a good cut, made him look taller. "And so patient with his niece," she mused aloud. "Our niece," she corrected herself, "he can be forgiven the hair."

Getting up from the floor, Mary headed over to her Mother. The sadness in her eyes made sense now. Her Mother may not see her, but the least she could do was put an arm around her. As she got close she realised she could still smell her, Mother smelled the same. She placed an arm across her Mother's shoulders, drinking in the warmth of her Mother's love.

"Ooh I got a shiver, is the door still open? Close it would you Alex?" Mother said.

Guilt wormed through Mary, "Sorry," she said as she moved away. Her mother had enough to deal with without Mary causing her shivers.

"Granny Catherine," Molly said. "Who's that lady?"

Mother and Lizzie looked at each other puzzled. "What lady sweetheart?" asked Lizzie.

"Don't be a silly button, Molly, there's no one here," Alex mocked.

"Yes, there is, she's right there, with her arm rounded on Granny Catherine," Molly stuck her tongue out at Alex as she pointed towards Mary.

Lizzie and Mother froze, shock etched on their faces. For a moment neither of them said or did anything, they couldn't move.

"You're seeing things silly noodle," laughed Alex.

Molly's face crumbled and tears began to fall at Alex's torment, "I'm not, I'm not," she stamped her feet in protest.

The children's banter brought Lizzie out of her stupor and she quickly gathered her thoughts and acted. "Alex go collect some eggs for tea, Molly come sit with Mummy at the table," she ordered.

Mother collapsed herself into the hearthside chair and stared at the fire, tears trickling down her cheeks.

Mary couldn't take her eyes off Molly. Molly could see her. Would she be able to hear her too?

Once Alex was out of the room Lizzie turned to Molly, passing her a handkerchief. "Now wipe your eyes and tell me, who is this lady Molly?"

Molly looked to the floor, her bottom lip stuck out and she didn't answer. The handkerchief sat unused in her hand.

"It's ok Molly, you aren't in any trouble. Just tell me about her," Lizzie said glancing at her Mother while chewing on a nail.

Mary had never seen Lizzie do that before. She used to have such beautiful nails.

"I'm not in trouble?" Molly looked doubtful.

Lizzie shook her head and smiled at her daughter, "no, I just want to know about her."

"Ok then," she wiped her eyes roughly, "well she's a lady

and she has brown hair, can I go and play now?" Molly moved as if to run off.

Lizzie smiled, but shook her head, "in a minute. Does she say anything?"

A puzzled look came over Molly's small face, her head dropped, and her lip stuck out again, "like what?"

Putting a finger under Molly's chin Lizzie lifted her head. "Don't look down, be proud and look at me. Just tell me if the lady says anything at all."

"Tell them my name is Mary-Mol and I am so sorry to make your Granny sad," Mary said. She hoped Molly could hear her and she hoped her mother wouldn't faint, she was looking decidedly pale.

Molly nodded and said, "Her name's Mary-Mol and she says she's sorry to make Granny Catherine sad. Can I go now Mummy, can I please?" Molly was sliding from the chair even as she asked.

Lizzie released her daughter with a nod, and as she dashed off outside shouting, "Uncle Alex wait for me," not giving it another thought, Lizzie found she was frozen to the spot.

She didn't speak, the blood drained from her face as her eyes scanned the room. Mary knew Lizzie couldn't see her, but she was obviously trying to. Minutes passed by, with neither Lizzie nor Mother moving or saying anything. A gasp and a sob from Mother brought Lizzie back to reality.

Mary wanted to be the one to comfort her mother, but she had to watch as Lizzie gulped and dashed to her Mother's side.

"Mother? Are you alright?" A shiver ran through her as she

moved, but her concern let her ignore it. It was obvious that Mother wasn't alright, her breath came in gasps and her face was wet and white as snow, with just a spot on each cheek as though Mary's blood had leaked there. Lizzie held her and they rocked together slowly until Mother's breathing settled.

Lizzie had walked right through Mary. Lizzie's shiver was nothing compared to the discomfort Mary felt. For Mary, it felt as though her insides had turned outside and nausea overwhelmed her. "Urgh, damn but that was awful." She knew she wasn't going to let that happen ever again. "I need to keep away from people."

Without young Molly there, Mary had no way of telling them anything, she could only listen and observe what was happening. She couldn't comfort her Mother, she couldn't talk to Lizzie. She was pretty much helpless and so frustrated. She wanted to help them, reassure them, but she could do nothing. She went to close the door, that much she could do or so she thought, but when she tried her hand went right through it.

"Damn and double damn, I can't do anything," Molly yelled as she slammed her hand against the door once more. This time the door shut. "Emotion? My anger lets me do things. Well, I have plenty of that so I shouldn't have much trouble."

Lizzie and Mother jumped as the door shut itself, but it was the final straw for Mother. The tears flowed and she sobbed on Lizzie's shoulder.

Guilt writhed through Mary and she felt herself squirm, she had frightened them and that was the last thing she wanted to do. What she really wanted was to hug her Mother and be hugged in return. She had come home expecting hugs and the security that a loving family gives, but there would be no more hugs for her. Not ever.

Diane Chesterton

Present Day

Diane Chesterton

Chapter 1

Molly gasped with horror as her Mother's ring slipped from her fingers, rolled across the old distorted oak flooring and headed for the gap in the floorboards.

Diving from the bed she raced after it, falling to her knees in a desperate bid to grab it before it disappeared.

"No, no, no!"

Peering through the gap, she could just make out the glint of gold. She had to get it back. It was all she had left of her Mum.

Gran kept a photo on the dresser downstairs, but that wasn't the same. Mum hadn't touched it or worn it. She knew it was foolish, but she was convinced she could sense her Mum just by touching the ring. No way was she leaving it under the floor.

Glancing around Gran's bedroom, she looked for anything that would help her. A double bed covered with a handmade quilt sat against a wall in the middle of the room. A chair by the side of it nursed Gran's knitting bag. Jumping to her feet she ran over, opened the bag, moved the ongoing project gently out of the way and grabbed the first needle she found.

Kneeling on the floor she peered into the hole. A glint of gold caught the light, but the ring itself seemed in darkness.

Prodding with the needle, she fumbled around until she looped the ring, but as the needle raised, the ring fell off.

"Poke the needle down the reverse way, stupid. Loop the ring over the blobby bit on the end. That should stop it from slipping off. A bit further." She had a habit of talking to herself and when she was in panic it was always worse. Gran said that men in white coats would take her away one day, but Molly was sure it was a joke. At least she hoped it was.

Biting her lower lip in concentration, Molly shuffled the needle this way and that, dragging it across the hole until she felt it slot through the ring. Slowly she lowered her side of the needle towards the floor and the ring raised up on the opposite side. She reached for the ring with her other hand as it lifted clear of the hole.

"Yes. Got it."

Grabbing the ring tight in her fist, she pulled the needle back across the floorboards out of the way of the hole, catching her hand on a splinter of wood sticking up in the process.

"Ow!"

Gripping the wound, she took a deep breath, not daring to look at the damage. Once before she'd cut herself, on a tin can. The sight of the cut had caused her to faint. That couldn't happen now.

Red sticky stuff leaked through her fingers. She knew the cut was bad, blood didn't flow so fast from a small nick.

Drip, drip.

She watched the blood seep through the gap in the floor, then a spark. Or was it a trick of the light? It happened so fast, it must have been.

Gripping the wound tight she could feel a slither of wood sticking out from the lower edge of her hand, it hurt like heck and made Molly nauseous and light-headed. She knew she needed Gran's help to get it out, she just had to make it downstairs.

Leaving the blood-covered needle where it was on the floor and placing the ring on the bedside table, Molly headed down the narrow, circular, wood stairs of the old cottage. She stopped holding the wound so she could grip the bannister tightly. The world started to spin.

"Mustn't faint, not on the stairs."

Taking deep, gasping breaths she made it to the bottom.

She could see Gran's salt and pepper hair bent over the kitchen worktop, making one of her arthritis concoctions for old Mr Lewis.

"Gran?" Molly called through clenched teeth.

On seeing Molly's ashen face and hands covered in blood Gran stopped in her tracks. "What happened?"

Hurriedly wiping sap off her hands on a white apron, she darted around the kitchen counter into the living room area of the cottage, just in time to catch Molly as the dizziness became too much, and she fainted.

She woke to see Gran leaning over her. The wood was gone from her hand and a bandage covered a healing compress, one of Gran's specialities. The scents of garlic and turmeric were unmistakable.

"You're ok now, do you want to tell me what happened?"

Gran said.

Molly looked down at the bandage, tears welling in her eyes. She always felt ashamed when she mentioned Mum to Gran. Like it was a betrayal of all Gran did for her. There was no escaping it this time though.

Between tears and hiccupping sobs, she explained how she'd been looking at Mum's ring, wanting that feeling of closeness she got from holding it. Wondering if she was still alive. How the ring had fallen through the gap in the wood and how she'd retrieved it. She didn't mention the spark she thought she'd seen when the blood dripped. It might not have happened after all, maybe just her imagination.

Molly had seen it before. Every time she mentioned Mum, Gran did the same thing. Shook her head with regret, wrapped her arms around Molly and held her tight, while combing back the long mousy brown hair that stuck to the tears on her face. Molly knew she was like her Mum. The photo on the cabinet proved it. A nose too small for her face and a mouth too large for the nose. She would never be called beautiful, but she misjudged the piercing green eyes indicative of spring grass that drew everyone's attention, leaving the flaws unnoticed.

"She's definitely alive, I promise you that," Gran said. "I'm sure she'll come back, we just need to be patient." Producing a tissue from her apron pocket Gran wiped away Molly's tears. "I know she must miss you terribly. She just has a few things to work out, grown-up things. It'll be ok."

Molly sobbed, "Why won't you tell me? If she's alive then why doesn't she come to see me? Am I such a wicked person that my own Mother doesn't want to see me?"

Gran sighed, "You're not a bad person Molly. This has nothing to do with you. I just need to be sure you're old enough to understand what's going on before I involve you. I always said that if she wasn't back when you reach your sixteenth birthday, I would tell you. It's not long to wait, just two months and then she's either here and can tell you herself or I will tell you."

They sat like that until Molly stopped crying, then Gran said, "Now I think you should go clean up the knitting needle, wash it in the bathroom sink and I'll get this potion done for old Mr Lewis. His arthritis's playing up again and modern medicine's all well and good, but nothing beats my old potion recipes."

As Molly rose from the sofa to head back up the stairs Gran added, "Take the ring and keep it in your room, then you can look at it whenever you wish."

With a grin Molly dashed back upstairs, the pain in her hand eased to almost nothing by the healing compress. In Gran's bedroom, she grabbed the ring and slotted it into her jeans pocket.

"I'll keep it safe for you Mum, I promise."

Picking up the knitting needle she headed to the bathroom to wash it clean. Over the sink, the bathroom mirror showed her tear-stained face.

"Bah stupid to cry, I'm sure she'll be back one day. I wish Gran would tell me where she is though. Why is it some big secret? I'm old enough now to understand. Wish she would realise that."

Picking up a face cloth she looked back at the mirror to clean away the tears. She saw her face looking back at her, but there was another face there too, someone behind her. Almost a double of Molly herself. Gripping the sink hard she closed her eyes and when she opened them the face was gone. She looked behind her, nothing. The bathroom was as it always had been and she was alone.

"Now I'm imagining things for sure. Come on Molly, get a grip and stop talking to yourself all the time. Folks'll think you're crazy."

She finished cleaning the needle, took it back to Gran's knitting bag and then headed to her room.

Painted in simple green with leaf-covered white curtains and bedding, it was instantly relaxing. Stuffed animals sat on a chair in a corner and at the end of her bed. The chest of drawers had clothing leaking out, preventing drawers from closing and the wardrobe was held open with shoes not properly tucked inside. Posters of nature and wildlife adorned the walls along with a solitary clock. Books were piled on top of a small bedside table and one, Herbs and their Uses, lay spread-eagled on her unmade bed.

Pulling the ring from her pocket she placed it carefully in her jewellery box on top of the chest of drawers. Not that she had much real jewellery, there wasn't any spare money for extravagances like that, mostly it was trinkets, but they were her trinkets and she wanted to keep them safe.

She knew Gran would want her to take the potion she'd

made to Mr Lewis, so she grabbed her trainers from under the bed and slipped them on, before heading downstairs.

"All done?" Gran asked from the sofa where she was idly flicking through a magazine, and without waiting for a reply added, "can you take that to Mr Lewis please." She pointed to a small bottle on the kitchen counter.

Nodding Molly reached for it, lifted her jean jacket from the hook near the door and slipped the bottle into a pocket. "Can I call and see Aisha?"

Glancing up with a smile Gran agreed, "Ok, lunch is at one, make sure you're back."

Molly bent and kissed Gran's cheek, "Thanks." Then she was out of the door and into a cloudy July's day, typical of the beginning of the school holidays.

She pulled the door behind her, failing to catch the latch. She'd just reached the wooden gate at the edge of the rose garden when she heard Gran call. "Close the door."

Grinning to herself she turned and headed back up the path. A shadow at Gran's bedroom window caught her eye and stopped her for a second, then it was gone. A shiver ran down her spine causing goosebumps to appear on her arms and chest. "Imagination going wild today," she muttered. After latching the door and another glance at the empty window, she was soon on her way to Mr Lewis's and to see Aisha.

Aisha lived on the other side of the village and Mr Lewis even further so it made sense to call for Aisha first. Heading down the street she glanced at the village green where mothers with young children were enjoying the open space, picnic blankets were laid and a rainbow of balls slipped from small fingers. Laughter filled the air and Molly smiled to herself. She could remember a time when she was one of those children and her Mum had the picnic blanket. She had been so secure thinking nothing in the world could touch her, not while Mum and Dad were around.

Continuing down the frequently trodden path she nodded and said, "good morning," to a new neighbour and waved to the elderly ones, the scents of cut roses and freshly hewn grass filled the air. Cloudy it may be, but it was still warm, she removed her jacket and slung it over a shoulder as she walked.

At the church, she glanced up towards the cemetery to whisper good morning to her Dad. She stopped for a moment and bowed her head, a ritual she had started just after his death, a form of remembrance. She was just about to set off again when she saw someone standing near his grave. Strangely dressed, but it looked like Molly herself. She blinked and the woman was gone. Glancing around she looked for the woman, but she had simply vanished. Irrational fear gripped her and she took off at a run.

She passed the garage with its mini supermarket, the odour of petrol and diesel hitting her nostrils, but not enough to stop her. Next was the newsagents which encompassed the post office run by old Mrs Cluck until a few years ago when she retired. Now her daughter, Rosie ran it. A safe place if she ever needed one, but still she didn't stop. Her heart pumped hard in her chest and she kept running. A quick scan of the road and she crossed over dashing passed the charity shop with not so much as a glance. She didn't stop until she reached the Marquis Arms, Aisha's home.

Glancing around, she saw nothing unusual, no shadows, no strange women. Taking a deep breath and wiping sweaty palms on her jeans, she berated herself for a stupid imagination, before stepping forward ignoring the 'no under 18's allowed' sign above her head and entering the pub.

Chapter 2

The pub was old with parts of it dating back to the Doomsday Book of 1086. It had stone walls and oak beams, seating and a bar. A red carpet covered the oak flooring. Scents of beeswax, stale ale and perfumes mixed to give the pub its unique aroma.

Over the years, the building had been added to, but the flat where Aisha lived was part of the original building. Going through the bar was the only way to get to the flat above the pub. Aisha's parents were working at the bar.

"Hi Mr and Mrs Darling, is Aisha in?"

Mr Darling smiled her way, "yes, just go on up Molly. She's on her computer as usual."

Molly nodded to the few customers in the bar as she passed through and headed up the stairs. Living in Colhome village all her life, she knew almost everyone.

This place hasn't changed much. Smells cleaner, but still the same.

"What?" Molly turned around on the stairs. "Who said that?"

There was no one there.

Treading slowly she headed back down towards the bar, looking for the speaker, but she saw no one.

He has a look of James, not so high and mighty now. Just another servant.

"Who's saying that?" Molly worried at her bottom lip

trying to make sense of what she was hearing. Feeling confused, she set off back upstairs, glancing behind her at each step.

The door at the top gaped open. Molly gave a small knock before pushing it wide and calling out, "Aisha, it's me, Molly, where are you?"

"In my bedroom Molly, won't be a sec. Just catching up on social media. Did you know Caitlyn's going out with Harry? She's stupid, he's only after one thing, then he'll dump her like all the rest."

Molly headed down a passage with doors leading off to the living areas. She glanced around looking for the owner of the strange voice, but saw no one. At the end of the passage was the door that led to Aisha's bedroom, where Molly found Aisha sitting at a desk busily clicking her mouse. Her petite blonde head didn't turn as Molly entered.

"Sit on my bed I won't be long," Aisha said.

Molly sat on a Harry Potter duvet. She really couldn't be bothered with Caitlyn and Harry today and the pettiness of it all. Caitlyn, was just one of many who tormented her in school. The leader of her own gang of what Gran would call, "Giggly little school girls." No one was as good as them and certainly not Molly. Her school bag had landed in the bin more than once by Caitlyn's hand. Then she and her 'gang' would stalk off laughing, looking for their next victim or some boy to leer at.

None of that stopped Caitlyn from asking for help in biology and expecting Molly to help though – after all, she was doing Molly a favour. Not everyone was allowed in the presence of the wonderful Caitlyn. As for Harry, he didn't know Molly existed, so she certainly wasn't going to worry about him.

It was the first day of the school holidays and in the first hour, she had wounded her hand, not an auspicious beginning. She was convinced she was losing it. Seeing shadows, faces, disappearing people and hearing voices. She had enough to consider without adding Caitlyn and Harry to the agenda. No, those two were not who she wanted to think about. "Not so sure who's most stupid, Caitlyn will take Harry for every penny he has then dump him. Maybe they deserve each other," she said.

"Woo," Aisha turned to look at Molly. "What got your goat this morning?"

Molly ignored the question, "I was wondering if you wanted to come with me to take a potion to Mr Lewis?"

"Sure, just a sec I'll turn this off and get my trainers."

Oooh, what is this magic? Your friend is a powerful sorceress? Typical Darling, accuse one person of witchcraft and they have one in their midst. Don't trust her.

Molly looked around, but she couldn't see anyone. "What are you talking about Aisha?"

"Me? I didn't say anything"

Goosebumps appeared again down Molly's arms. If Aisha didn't say it, then who did? The mysterious voice again? She looked under the bed, getting down on her knees to have a better look. No-one there. Maybe when she fainted she really did hit her head? That would explain it. It was only since then that she had seen and heard things.

Aisha looked wide-eyed at Molly as she ferreted under the

bed, "What are you doing? Did you lose something?"

Looking up guiltily Molly blushed and asked, "Are you ready? Can we go?"

With a sideways glance at Molly, Aisha said "Yes." Then as an afterthought, "Are you ok?"

Molly nodded and led the way towards the exit from the flat, chewing on her bottom lip as she went.

Aisha locked the door before they headed down the stairs and out through the Marquis Arms.

"Going out with Molly," Aisha called to her parents and anyone else in earshot. "I've got my mobile if you need me."

Mr and Mrs Darling waved to the back of the girls' heads as they disappeared outside.

"Come on," Molly said. "Let's go through the woods it'll be quicker." She didn't just want to be quick, she wanted to leave the Marquis Arms as fast as possible. Those voices had her scared.

Running, they went through the pub carpark, waited for a solitary car to pass then crossed the road to the entrance to the woods, a mud path.

"I'm glad you called for me," Aisha said at last. " I needed to talk to you and I didn't want to do it over the phone."

"Why, what's up?"

Molly waited while Aisha took a moment before answering.

This is where a Darling betrays you. They always do you know. You can't trust a Darling.

Molly looked around, but she could see nothing other than trees, birds, and squirrels. The colour drained from her face, her heart raced. Was she going nuts? Had she really done some damage to her head when she fainted? Lost in her thoughts she only just caught the last part of what Aisha said. That they wouldn't see each other hardly at all.

"What!? Why won't we see each other?" Molly had totally missed everything, but she didn't miss the look on Aisha's face that said, you're not listening to me, what on Earth is wrong with you?

Aisha repeated slowly and carefully, as though Molly was a five-year-old, "The brewery. Is renovating, the Marquis. Particularly the flat. Mum and Dad say. They can make do downstairs. I have to go, stay with my Nan. I will be in Scotland. For the whole holidays. They won't let me stay. I leave tomorrow. Did you understand?"

Ok, so not a betrayal. But she is leaving you.

"No, Aisha you can't. It's all going wrong. I need you. Can't you stay with me? You could sleep in my room."

Molly waited while Aisha looked at her, really looked. The bandage on her hand. The paleness of her face. Tears welling in her eyes. The recollection of the strange behaviour in her bedroom. "Tell me on the way to Mr Lewis's," Aisha said.

Ah, now she wants to know. She'll still leave you, you know. Everyone does.

"Shut up, you know nothing. Leave me alooonnne," Molly shouted.

Aisha stopped. Her eyes widened and her mouth dropped open in surprise. "I really am sorry Molly. I knew you wouldn't be happy, but that is a bit over the top. I'll go though, I'm sure I can find someone else to spend my last day in Colhome with."

"What? No, I wasn't talking to you Aisha." She grabbed Aisha by the arm. "Please, don't go, I need you. I'll try to explain. Come on, let's sit on the fallen oak."

Pulling a reluctant Aisha towards the decaying log Molly sat and patted the log at her side. After checking for termites and ants Aisha sat.

Gazing at the bandage on her hand Molly told the story of her strange morning. She didn't look at Aisha. She didn't want to see if Aisha thought she was totally round the twist. She couldn't bear the thought that her best friend, her only friend, might not want to see her anymore. They had been friends since they were babies. Aisha had been there for her when her dad died and her mum disappeared. The other kids didn't know what to say to her and slowly she became an outcast, someone different. The one without parents. What do you say to someone like that? The fact that she shrank into a shell and withdrew from them all didn't help either.

So now she only had one friend, Aisha. But who would want to be friends with a crazy girl? Aisha may not be her friend when she realised Molly had lost the plot. Molly didn't know what she would do without Aisha to lean on. She finished her story and waited for Aisha to say something. She didn't glance up, even as Aisha spoke.

"So you really weren't talking to me? Just to some invisible voice in your head?"

Molly glanced at Aisha and was relieved to see her friend didn't look appalled or frightened. "Yes. Do you think I'm going crazy?"

"You've always been crazy girl," Aisha laughed.

Molly pushed her sideways in retaliation, "I'm not the only crazy one here you know."

"You prefer animals to people and plants to technology. How crazy is that?" Aisha continued

"Oh, and building your own pc is not crazy? You could have bought one so much cheaper and easier," Molly retorted. How they could be best friends since they were babies Molly never understood. They were as different as chalk and cheese, but Aisha was like family to her and their differences didn't seem to matter.

Aisha grinned, "No way could I buy one as good as mine, it would cost a small fortune. Anyway, we were talking about you. It could be that you banged your head. If this strangeness continues you might need to get checked out by a doctor. The spark you saw though, that's odd, it's worth investigating. You need to look under the floorboard. I bet there's something there. Your cottage is as old as the Marquis Arms, who knows what secrets it holds."

Molly considered for a moment then nodded, "you could be right. Let's get this potion to Mr Lewis, then if you have time we could look together."

"This is going to be fun. Now I really wish I wasn't going to Nan's. I asked if I could come to yours, but Mum said it's for too long and not fair to your Gran. We can still chat on the phone though."

"If you hear me talking strange, be sure I'm not talking to

you," Molly said. Then she grinned, "it will just be my invisible, not-so-friendly friend."

Hey, I heard that.

Molly had sounded brave talking to Aisha, but hearing the voice again made her insides recoil. She thought she might be sick. No, she couldn't be sick. They would figure this out, find out what was going on. Swallowing the extra saliva that washed her mouth she headed after Aisha who had already set off in the direction of Mr Lewis'.

She was fairly sure she wasn't imagining things. Aisha hadn't poopooed the idea at all. There was something going on and it had a lot to do with the spark after the blood fell through the floorboards.

Mr Lewis lived on the edge of the woods in a compound with other older people. His wife had died many years ago and although he had children they had long since left Colhome and he rarely saw them.

He watched Molly and Aisha arriving through his open window and called to them. "Come in the door's open."

He sat in an armchair with a leg raised on a stool. A bandage covered his calf. It looked clean and obviously new. The scent of antiseptic filled the air.

"Got you your potion Mr Lewis," Molly said. "Gran sends her regards."

"Bless her, she's a good soul. Thank you Molly."

"What happened to your leg?" Molly asked.

"Oh, nothing much. I banged it on the dresser. It'll be fine.

Nurse comes every day and checks it. Don't ya go worrying yer Gran about it, I know how she likes to fix everyone up. If I need her I'll shout, don't ya worry. Money for the potion is on the dresser and there's some Twix bars in the top drawer, get yerself one and one for young Aisha too. Would yer other friend like one?"

Molly looked around, "other friend?"

"Yes the one hiding in the corner, come out child I don't bite, I had my breakfast today and children are not my favourite meal."

Molly felt goosebumps reappear across her back and down her arms. She looked in the corner where Mr Lewis pointed. There was definitely a shadow there, for just a moment. Then it was gone.

"Strange, I was sure I saw someone," said Mr Lewis. "Must be these old eyes playing tricks."

"No, just us," said Aisha. "Thanks for the Twix Mr Lewis. See ya."

Aisha grabbed Molly by the arm, "Come on Molly, we need to look at that thing you mentioned."

"Ah yes. Bye Mr Lewis, thanks for the Twix. Hope your leg's better soon."

Once outside, Molly turned to Aisha, "did you see it?"

"No, but Mr Lewis obviously did. That means you're not losing your marbles. Come on, we need to find out what's under your floorboards."

Chapter 3

Molly and Aisha raced through the woods. Slipping on mud from the previous day's rain and tumbling over ancient roots of oak, elm and ash trees. They didn't stop until they reached the centre.

"Stop Aisha. Why are we running?"

"Erm, well, 'cos we want to find out what's under the floorboards of course," Aisha replied

"We don't need to run though. Tell you what, I'll ask Gran if you can stay for lunch, then we can have all day together. Lots of time to work out what's going on."

Oooh, friendsy, friendsy. She's leaving you. She'll have a new friend soon.

"Oh shut up whoever you are, leave me alone."

Aisha gave Molly a sideways glance, "I hope that's your invisible friend you're talking to."

"Yeh, she never shuts up yammering in my ear. Whoever she is I think she wasn't very happy. That's probably why she's still here."

"Maybe we could work out who it could be if we… what's that your Gran says? Put our thinking caps on?" Aisha said.

"Yes, thinking caps. Not sure what one would look like," Molly replied with a laugh.

"It started in your cottage Molly, so whoever it is, has a tie to the cottage. We just have to think about who used to live there."

"You're right." Molly stopped walking and turned to Aisha. "The cottage has been in my family since forever. It's Gran's now, but it was her Mum's before that and so on. So the chances are she's a relative."

Oh, little miss clever clogs now.

Molly ignored the voice. "The other thing she's about 15 or 16 same as us, maybe just a bit older, or at least the face I saw in the mirror looked our age."

"Good. We know a bit more now. Someone female, about 15 or 16 and a relative of yours." Aisha said. "Maybe when we find whatever is under the floorboards we'll have our answer. Then we need to figure out how to send her back to wherever she came from."

Feeling happier all the time, with Aisha to show her some common sense and the scents from the woods soothing her, Molly relaxed. The voice couldn't hurt her, even the shadow couldn't do her any damage. What was she so worried about anyway. It was just like having an annoying little sister tagging along behind her. Or at least that's what she imagined it would be like. She could deal with this.

A huge oak tree blocked their way.

"Oh we were so busy talking we must have taken the wrong path," Molly said. "Let's go around it, we'll be able to see the cottage from the other side. This tree is huge, Gran says it's the oldest tree in the woods."

Ancient and sad. Get away from it. This way.

Molly looked up and found she could see a shadow leading

them away from the tree. Taking a deep breath to keep herself calm she said, "seems my invisible friend also knows the way. Come on Aisha."

"You can see her?" Aisha whispered, as though there was some secret they were keeping from the ghost.

Molly nodded, "just a shadow," she said as she stumbled after the shadow, following an old disused path. Carefully pushing aside nettles, ferns and cowslip they were soon back on the usual trail. The shadow had vanished and through the gap in the trees, Molly and Aisha could see the cottage. A gate in the fence let them into the garden at the back.

The gate had been there as long as Molly could remember, they used it when they needed to gather herbs from the woods for Gran's potions. Mostly it was Gran that did the gathering, but sometimes she would send Molly. Molly liked it best when they went together and Gran would teach her about the different plants and their uses. Molly kept a notebook with drawings and details of all the plants Gran taught her about. She hoped it would be useful when she went to university to study botany.

Today though, the thought of plants was at the back of her mind. The shadow and the voice were more important.

"I guess I could say she's my Ghost?" Molly said.

"Which means, your cottage is haunted. Wow, Molly, you live in a haunted cottage."

"Shh, don't let Gran hear. I wouldn't want to worry her."

Entering the cottage through the back stable-type door, the smell of ham cooking on the stove made their mouths water.

Gran was just pouring pasta into a pan ready to boil.

"Ah, good timing Molly, lunch is nearly ready. You want to stay for lunch Aisha?"

Aisha nodded eagerly. It smelled delicious and if she didn't stay she would have to make do with a jam sandwich. When the Marquis closed her Mum would make them dinner, but that was ages away. Staying at Molly's was definitely preferable. "I'll phone Mum and tell her I'm stopping here."

After Aisha had made her phone call, she and Molly set the table and they sat down to delicious ham and pasta with cheese. While they ate, Molly suggested to Gran that maybe she saw something below the floorboards in her room and asked if it would be ok for them to look. She knew Gran wouldn't be impressed if she and Aisha just invaded her bedroom without asking.

"Ok," said Gran, "but don't go making a mess. And if you do, clean it up!"

"Yes Gran, promise."

Molly and Aisha grinned at each other. The puzzle will soon be solved.

You think it is that simple huh? You don't know the half of it yet.

Molly ignored the voice. She could see the shadow slumped on the sofa, it seemed to have more form, more like what she'd seen in the mirror. It was becoming less shadow, more solid. She glanced from Aisha to Gran, but neither of them seemed to notice.

"Leave the pots, I'll see to them," Gran said, and don't forget, no mess."

"Yes, Gran."

"Yes, Mrs Barber."

The two friends raced up the stairs to Gran's room.

"Here's where the ring dropped," said Molly pointing at the floorboard.

Kneeling down they peered into the hole. It was too small for their fingers to explore and too dark to see anything.

"We need a torch." Aisha looked around as if one would miraculously appear.

"I have one in my room." Molly dashed out and was back in seconds. The torch beamed brightly. Pointing it at the hole they stared down.

"Is that a book?" Molly asked, looking at Aisha bewildered. "Why would a book be down there? And how can we possibly get it out."

Glancing around the bedroom for inspiration it dawned on Molly that the Ghost was missing. She'd gotten so used to her being there, that it seemed strange without her. No voice, no shadow. Well, maybe it was a good thing. They didn't want distractions while they tried to figure out what was happening and why the Ghost was there in the first place.

Aisha was standing again, looking around. "There must be a means of getting the floorboard up. If the book was put down there, then there had to be a way the owner expected to get it back."

"Of course. This cottage is very old though, maybe things changed over time. Who knows how old the book might be." Molly looked around, "I'm thinking."

Aisha sat on Gran's bed. She still looked around, but there was nothing obvious and Molly was always better at puzzles than she was. Molly would work it out.

"I really don't know," Molly said.

Aisha pulled her phone from her jeans pocket, "Let me check Google. It might give us a clue."

Molly moved to the side of Aisha on Gran's bed and watched as Aisha typed in, 'how to unlock a secret compartment.'

Looking up from the phone, her eyes shining, Aisha said, "There should be a switch somewhere. Somewhere not too obvious."

They looked around but there was nothing that even resembled a switch. No bookcases with a book to move. No panels that needed pressing. Nothing. Molly chewed on her lip as she pondered and Aisha searched Google for more ideas.

"No hints on Google sorry."

"My bedroom's next to Gran's, let's go look there." Slipping the torch into her jeans pocket she led the way to her bedroom.

"What do you think we should look for? It's your room you know it well. Is there anything you ever wondered about?"

Molly chewed her lip as she considered then gasped, "Actually, yes. Do you see how there's a little alcove near the skirting board on the wall adjoining Gran's room? I always wondered why that was there. Let's investigate it."

Sitting side by side on the floor they glared at the alcove. Aisha prodded it carefully. Nothing happened. Molly tapped it with her fingers. Still nothing.

They looked at each other and said together, "I don't know." This started them giggling. The giggles turned to laughter.

"Why are we laughing?" Molly splurted between laughing fits.

"I don't know, but it's funny anyway." Aisha laughed some more.

"I got a belly ache now," Molly said as she hiccupped to quietness.

"Yeh, me too. Feel better for that though. My brain's working better. Feel around the inside of the alcove Molly. See if there's a switch or something."

Molly did as Aisha suggested, running her fingers around the inside of the alcove, over the top and sides. "Nope, nothing. Hang on I'll press around it, see if that's how it works."

Carefully Molly used her fingers to press everywhere. "No, nothing. Big fail. You have a try." Resting her hand on the inside of the alcove Molly lifted herself to her knees and then pressed the alcove to help her stand up.

"Did you hear that Molly? I heard a catch click. What did you do?"

"I just used the alcove to help me stand up. I pressed my hand against it."

Without another word, the girls ran back into Gran's bedroom and stopped. The whole of one floorboard was missing. Pulling the torch back out of her jeans pocket Molly shone it towards the gap in the floor.

"Come on Molly, it's like opening a treasure chest. I wonder what we'll find."

Molly didn't move.
She stood and stared.
It wasn't just a shadow that appeared in front of her.
It was a girl.

Chapter 4

It was almost like looking in a mirror, the clothes were different, a long skirt and bodice. The hair was pinned up under a bonnet, but it was the same mousy brown as Molly's. It was the look on her face that had the biggest effect.

Eyes of emerald green were angry. Wide and staring. Glaring at Aisha.

Her mouth turned down in a sneer, lips thin and so pale almost bloodless.

Her hands were balled into fists. Molly had the distinct impression the Ghost was about to hit someone or something. Probably Aisha.

Trembling, Molly covered her mouth to stop the scream that wanted to rip from her lungs. Backing away from the hole towards the door and escape, she couldn't take her eyes off the Ghost.

"Aisha, don't move."

Aisha didn't listen. She moved towards the hole, walking straight through the Ghost.

"Ooh I got a shiver, that was strange, I'm covered in goosebumps."

She's not your friend, she'll betray you. It's in her blood.

Molly ignored the words of the Ghost in front of her.

Aisha's voice broke the spell that seeing the form of the Ghost had cast over Molly. The Ghost's voice was the same one she'd heard all day. The shadow had been there, now it had a form. It was not happy, it obviously had issues and for some reason, those issues were with Aisha. She walked towards Aisha and the hole, dismissing the Ghost.

"Go away, Aisha is my friend. I don't know you."

"The shadow again?" Aisha asked.

"Not a shadow anymore. I can see her."

"You can? What does she look like? Is she small and pretty like me or tall and lanky like you?"

"Cheeky minx." Molly couldn't help laughing even as she considered her answer. She couldn't tell Aisha about the anger, so she just said, "she's a lot like me."

"I bet she's your relative, some ancestor from long ago. Maybe she wants to know about computers, they wouldn't have them in the olden days."

"I don't think she's here to look at computers Aisha. Anyway, she's gone now. Come on let's see if something beneath the floorboards can give us a clue."

Bending to the floor and shining the torchlight into the hole, the two girls peered in. There was definitely a book. It was small, almost like a notepad with a soft leather cover. Gently Molly lifted it out. It felt delicate. She opened it carefully. The pages were yellow with age and fragile. She closed it, placed it on the floor beside her and peered back down the hole, flashing the torchlight around to see what else she could see.

Spiders webs everywhere.

"Yuk," said Aisha. "I hate spiders."

"They won't hurt you. Lots of spiders live in houses, under

the floorboards and everywhere. Where would you rather live? Inside or out? Anyway, these are just webs, the spiders will have run away when the floor opened."

"Ok I know, but it doesn't mean I have to like them and webs are so sticky. Yuk, yuk, yuk."

Molly grinned as she swept the webs out of the way with her hand and wiped the sticky residue on her jeans.

She peered once more into the hole flashing her torch everywhere.

"What's that?" Aisha asked.

"Where?"

"There." Aisha pointed into a distant corner where she could see a glint of something.

Lying flat on the floor so she could reach further, Molly stretched her arm towards the corner Aisha had pointed to. The tips of her fingers scrailed something cold and hard. Inching forward on her belly she tried again. This time she managed to grab it, clasping it tightly in her hand she edged back away from the hole and sat on her heels. Opening her hand she and Aisha looked with excitement at what it could be.

"A pocket watch?" they said in unison.

"Why would someone hide a pocket watch?" Aisha said.

"No idea."

Leave it alone, it's not yours. Just another betrayal. Why do you poke around in things that are not your business?

The pocket watch flew from Molly's hand, sliding across the floor to rest under Gran's bed.

Falling back in surprise Molly almost hit her head on the

bedpost, while Aisha went white, her mouth dropping open in disbelief.

"Guess the Ghost is not too happy we found that," Molly said as she pulled herself back to her original sitting position near the hole.

Pushing a hand under her chin to close her mouth, Aisha could only nod. It was the first time she had actually felt the presence of the Ghost. Now she understood more how confused Molly must have been all morning.

"Let's check there isn't anything else under the floor then we can get the watch back," Molly said, with more composure than she felt.

Peering into the hole once more they looked to see if they could find anything else, but there was just blackness glaring back at them. A quick ferret under Gran's bed soon had the pocket watch back in Molly's hands. She stuffed it into her jeans pocket, no way was she letting the Ghost take it from her again.

"I'll close the floorboard from my room then I think we should show these to Gran, she might know something about them."

Tumbling down the stairs in excitement they had to grab the bannister to stop a serious fall.

"Hey, you two be careful. My healing potions are good, but not so good they can heal broken bones," Gran said moving to sit at the table. Resting her elbows on the table she used her hands to prop her head up before asking, "So what did you find?"

Things they had no right to touch.

Molly looked around, the Ghost was sitting on a stool at the kitchen counter, looking more sullen and angry than ever. She tried to ignore her, biting her lip to stop herself from looking that way, but it was difficult. The Ghost was still glaring at Aisha as if it were all Aisha's fault.

Deliberately turning her back on the Ghost, Molly said, "We found a notebook and a pocket watch, look."

They're not yours, put them back.

"Bring them to the table, let's see if we can tell why they were hidden. Oh, and I made fresh lemonade if you want to help yourself." Gran nodded towards a glass jug on the counter.

Molly headed to the table and placed the two items in the centre, before heading to the counter where Aisha was just pouring out the lemonade into two glasses. Taking a glass each they sipped the lemonade as they joined Gran at the table, to examine the bounty they had found.

At first, they all just looked at them. Then Gran picked up the notebook, turning it in her hands to examine it. A musty smell met their nostrils as she manoeuvred it around.

"This used to be called a pocketbook or commonplace book," she said. "People would write in them with charcoal, there were no pencils or ballpoint pens and only the rich had ink." Opening it gently she laid the book on the table so they all could see. The yellowed pages were covered in drawings of different plants with brief explanations underneath. Further on recipes were listed for healing or poisoning, depending on the doses. As they looked quickly through they found dates listed and it became more like a diary than a notebook.

"We should read this slowly later. There could be recipes I don't know in there," said Gran. "I'll copy them out so I can use them. The book is far too old for regular use. It looks to be the diary of a girl about your age Molly. Strange, because girls weren't taught to read and write back then. It was thought we didn't have the brains for it."

Molly and Aisha looked at each other and burst out laughing. "What did they think? That girls were stupid or what?" Molly said with a grin.

Gran smiled and tapped her nails repetitively on the table before answering. "No, not stupid, but a lot of people thought it a waste. They believed girls were only good for making babies and looking after the home and men. It was what was expected. Women and girls stayed at home, men were in charge and needed knowledge. Women had very few rights, they were basically the property of men. Why do you think women are given away at a wedding ceremony? It's not as romantic as it sounds, it's about ownership." Gran glanced up at the two girls and couldn't help a chuckle at their wide eyes. "This will make interesting reading. 1645, that's so long ago it will be an education for us all. Now let's look at the pocket watch."

Molly nodded, she wanted to take the diary and start reading immediately. Maybe it would provide answers about her Ghost, but she would have to be patient. The pocket watch needed looking at too. Glancing to the kitchen counter she could see the Ghost still sat scowling in their direction. At least she was quiet for the moment.

"Hey, I just Googled pocket watches. Girls didn't have

them, only boys. So it must belong to a boy," Aisha announced.

Molly and Gran couldn't help but laugh. If Aisha wanted to know anything, she was always there with Google.

"Let's look at it shall we and then make some assumptions?" Gran said.

The pocket watch had a glass front showing the time, small flowers painted delicately around the sides. It looked like the base was made from gold, Gran hunted for a hallmark then stopped. "Stupid me, gold wasn't stamped in the long and distant past, but there is something written on the back."

Molly

My friend

Both Gran and Aisha looked at Molly. Molly looked at the Ghost.

So my name's Molly, so what! It's actually Mary, only Molly to my friends.

"Looks like the watch belongs to you Molly," Aisha grinned, but Gran was more serious.

"We should put these things safe," said Gran. "Maybe you could walk Aisha home Molly. I'm sure her mum will want her to get her things together ready to go to her nan's tomorrow. It's almost tea time and she won't have much time before bed. Have a lovely trip Aisha, see you when you get back." Gran rose from the table, took the book and the pocket watch and locked them away in the dresser drawer.

"But Gran?" Molly was confused. What just happened?

Your Gran knows. She knows the watch is mine. The notebook is mine. She knows.

Glancing at the Ghost, Molly was incensed. "Gran, Aisha has loads of time, why does she have to go now? It's not fair."

Gran raised her eyebrows. A glacier stare at Molly. Molly was silenced.

Aisha was confused too, but she knew marching orders when she heard them. "Thanks for lunch Mrs Barber. See you when I get back."

"Bye Aisha. Straight back Molly," Gran said.

As soon as they were out of earshot Molly grabbed Aisha's arm spinning her around so they faced each other. "What on earth was that about," she said. "Gran was rude to you and, she locked the things away. I can't even get to them anymore."

"Hey calm down Molly, it's ok. She was right, it is time I went home and maybe she didn't want me around when she tells you whatever it is she knows. You can tell me later anyway. I'll be on the phone with you every day and you can text me."

"I don't even know where my phone is," Molly said. "I'll find it out, I'm going to need it I guess."

"You really should use it more often. At least take it with you when you go out. You are totally living in the 1900s. Get with the program Molly, everyone uses a mobile nowadays." Aisha grinned to take the sting out of her words.

"I know," said Molly, "but they're bulky and with all the stuff I do in the woods, well it's not practical. It's not like I would use it anyway. Who would I phone? There's only you and I can walk to yours to chat with you." Molly could see the resignation on Aisha's face. They'd had this conversation many times, but Molly wasn't going to change her mind. She didn't feel the need for a phone. Linking her arm through Aisha's she dragged her friend along. "Come on, we can go the long way around through the woods. It'll give us time together."

Reverting to the back of the cottage they headed into the woods.

"The woods always calm me. I love the smell of damp earth, moss and trees. I'm sure Gran has a good reason for doing what she did. We should enjoy this last day together, not stress over Ghost Mary, Molly or whatever she likes to be called," Molly said.

"You think the Ghost is the Molly on the watch?" Aisha asked.

"I don't think, I know. She just about told me while we were looking at the stuff. But we have to call her Mary, only Molly to her friends she said."

"Really? Wow, that's awesome." Aisha looked around then back over her shoulder, "Is she here now?"

Molly did a quick glance around, "No. Thank goodness. She really seems to not like you Aisha. I don't know why."

"Maybe it's not me, but some memory I make her think of? Should I Google it?"

"No! For heaven's sake don't. Put your phone away. I swear you have an umbilical cord attached to it. Google doesn't have the answer to everything you know," Molly said. Anyway, do ghosts do association?" she found the idea curious. "We make assumptions about ghosts, but no one really knows anything."

"Well, I've never heard of anyone actually seeing a Ghost before, that's because you're special Molly. I have a special friend," Aisha grinned cheekily then ducked as Molly made to hit her with the piece of grass she'd been chewing. Aisha wasn't done tormenting though, "see how special you are, eating grass like a cow."

"That's it, come here you."

Seeing that Molly looked serious, Aisha set off running through the woods, laughter rippled behind her. Molly chased after her. "Get back here, I'll make you pay for that, cow indeed." Then she too started to laugh, and they ran on with laughter ringing through the trees.

All too soon they reached the edge of the woods. Across the road, the Marquis Arms stood waiting to swallow Aisha and spit her out the next day to stay with her Nan in Scotland.

"I'm going to miss you Aisha, phone me every day and I'll give you an update, let you know the progress with our ghost friend."

"You can be sure of it and if you need anything researching send me a text and I can Google it for you."

Molly sighed, "Of course you can."

The two friends hugged each other, and then Aisha was across the road and waving as she entered the pub.

Turning back to the woods Molly started a slow walk home.

Good riddance to bad rubbish I say.

"Go away!"

Oh, I'll go alright. Right to the Darling's home. It's time I fixed this myself.

"Wait, what? No. Leave Aisha and her family alone." She looked around, but there was no sign of the Ghost. She could only hope the Ghost couldn't really hurt them. Should she warn them? Well, Aisha already knew about the Ghost and she was sure Mr and Mrs Darling wouldn't believe her. Probably best to leave it. She needed to get home anyway.

She needed answers from Gran, not more secrets. She felt like she was surrounded by secrets. How she wished her Mum would come back, maybe then the secrets would stop. She was sure she wouldn't feel so lost if her Mum hadn't disappeared. She would have been able to ask Mum things that she wasn't comfortable asking Gran about.

"I'm sure Mum wouldn't have locked the things in the drawer and sent Aisha away. She would have listened and included us in everything."

Really she had no idea how her Mum would have reacted, but in her head she could romanticise, imagine them with the perfect mother-daughter relationship. Cooking together, laughing together, movies and popcorn together. She knew she was being unfair to Gran when she daydreamed of her Mum, but she couldn't help it. She felt more alone than she had since the day her Mum had left.

"On grown-up business, is all Gran ever says. Whatever that is. Why won't she tell me?" Molly felt frustrated and angry. She kicked the loose soil underfoot until her toe hit a stone and she yelped in surprise. She went back to her musings, a thing she did more often lately, testing her memory to see if it gave her any answers. It never did, but she had to try.

Grown-up business had started on the same day her Dad had had his accident. The last she could remember of Mum was the sobbing and screaming when she knew Dad had gotten up early and quietly gone to work, without disturbing them. Why that would upset her Molly had no idea. He frequently went to work early. On this day though, Mum had been hysterical, beyond reasoning with. Molly had only been eight, she didn't know what to do about it, and she needed to get to school. So she'd called Gran to come over. She didn't know what she would have done without Gran since that day.

Gran had been like an angel. She calmed Mum down, got Molly ready for school and dropped her at the school gate. When Mrs Darling dropped her home after school that evening as usual, the police were waiting. Her Mum had gone, no one would tell her where, and her Dad had been killed in a car accident.

Gran had been a rock for the younger Molly. Just eight years old and both parents gone. But Gran said Mum would be back. She just had to be patient.

Since that day Gran had helped Molly through everything. She was usually kind and thoughtful, rarely shouting or being abrupt. It was so unlike her to push Aisha away, or to lock something away that Molly had found. Nothing was adding up to the Gran she knew. When she got home she would ask what it was all about. She needed answers.

Chapter 5

*E*veryone *betrays you, you know.*
Molly ignored the Ghost. It was walking beside her, skirt swinging, silently brushing the undergrowth. Solid in a not reassuring way. Molly had preferred the shadow, at least she didn't feel like she was looking in a mirror each time she caught sight of it. The fact that the Ghost was there meant she hadn't gone over to The Marquis Arms. Molly felt a sigh of relief. She still had time to find out what was going on and get rid of the Ghost.

They keep secrets from you, everyone does. Your Gran has secrets. Bet she didn't tell you where your Mum is. I know. I know everything. It sends you nuts when you know everything. You should ask your Gran, but she won't tell you.

"Shut up and go away, will you? You know nothing. You don't know me, you don't know Aisha and you don't know Gran. Just leave me alone." Molly was close to tears, everything was going wrong and the Ghost was just rubbing it in. Molly knew nothing. She was treated like a child. But she wasn't a child anymore. It was time she was treated more like an adult and trusted.

Sitting on the soft moss in the middle of the woods she let the tears trickle slowly down her face. It was the summer holidays when she should be having fun, but all she had was a Ghost that wouldn't leave her alone. Aisha gone or at least going. Mum gone and Gran not telling her anything. She knew the Ghost was right, Gran was keeping secrets. Gran had always kept secrets.

Molly sat and sat. She sniffed the tears that made her nose run, then as if to add to her misery cool rain fell through the branches of the trees. The scent of wet moss and foliage grew stronger as the rain fell harder and started to bounce, she was wet through, her hair stuck to her head, her jeans stuck to her legs, but she didn't move.

"Well Molly Barber are you just going to sit here full of self-pity and getting soaked, or are you going to come home, get dried and we can talk," Gran said.

Molly looked up, Gran stood over her, umbrella in hand, a welcome shelter against the downpour. She didn't get up. She didn't know if she wanted to talk to Gran. Gran had sent Aisha home. Their last day together and Gran had cut it short.

"Sulking and feeling sorry for yourself will not provide answers. Come along now and bring some of that wild garlic with you, I'm running short."

Gran handed Molly a tissue, turned and walked away, taking the umbrella with her. After wiping her eyes Molly raised herself from the sodden moss floor, blew her nose with a tissue that was wetter from rain than from tears, grabbed the wild garlic that Gran had pointed out and set off after her. Looking around there was no sign of the Ghost. "One good thing anyhow."

Talking to yourself? That's the first sign.

Molly ignored the voice.

By the time Molly entered the cottage she was dripping from head to toe. Water fell from her jeans to the floor, her trainers squelched with each step and her hair was lank and lifeless.

"Go get changed, I'll have some chamomile tea waiting when you get down, then we can talk," Gran said.

Molly trudged upstairs, stripped off her wet clothes in the bathroom, careful not to look in the mirror. She didn't want reminding of the Ghost. After drying herself and rubbing briskly at her hair she was soon in warm clothes and headed back down to hot tea and toast, with lashings of butter and jam. She would rather have had hot chocolate, but she knew the chamomile would calm her down so she didn't complain.

Sitting at the table she drank and ate quietly waiting for Gran to start talking. On the edge of her vision, she could see a shadow. Ghost Mary was there, but for some reason not wanting to show herself. That was fine with Molly, she didn't want to see her.

Gran sat across from Molly, took a sip of her tea and began to talk.

"Normally your Mum would talk to you about this. I really hoped she would be back so she could be with you at this time. Unfortunately, you found the book and the watch and need to know some information." She took a breath and another sip of tea. "I won't tell you everything, some things you can wait to find out, but this is important now."

Molly was all ears, maybe now Gran would tell her where her mum was. She was sure Gran was stalling. She seemed to be saying anything except the stuff that really mattered. Her chamomile tea was done, and the toast half eaten sat lonely on her plate. She looked Gran in the eye and waited, biting her lip in anticipation.

Getting up from her seat Gran went over to the dresser drawer, unlocked it and retrieved the book and watch. Placing the items in the centre of the table she sat down and sipped again at her tea.

"The watch says Molly on the back," Gran said. "Molly was born in 1630 and died in 1645. Actually, she was murdered in 1645. Her real name was Mary, but she was frequently called Molly. It's not used nowadays, but back then, Marys were often called Molly by family and friends."

A quick glance where the shadow had been, showed Molly that the Ghost was listening. She was more solid now, seeming to concentrate on Gran. A look of satisfaction stole her face when Gran said she was murdered.

Looking back to Gran, Molly waited for her to continue.

"A lot of the facts have been lost across the years, but what I do know is, she was the sister of my great-great-great, so many greats you don't need to know, grandmother."

"So she's a relative?" Molly asked.

Gran nodded, "a distant one, but yes. Anyway, she took a potion to some friend of her mothers who was having a baby. Long story short, the mother and baby died and for some reason, she was blamed. It was the time of the witch hunts, you know about those?"

Molly knew some things, what she had seen on tv and stuff

but not a great deal. She shrugged and waited for Gran to continue.

"Any woman not conforming to what people thought normal could be called a witch. Mary didn't conform to much. She would talk to herself a lot and the townsfolk were suspicious, saying that she was talking to the Devil. She was what was known as a wild child, always in the woods behind the cottage, not worrying about her appearance too much." Gran grinned at Molly, "I guess you two were much alike."

If only Gran knew Molly thought. It's like looking in a mirror to look at her. It didn't make any sense though. Why would Ghost Mary think she was betrayed? It was the suspicious townsfolk that were against her, not just one person. Should she ask Gran? But Gran was talking again.

"After the mother and baby died, a mob came to this cottage." Seeing the look of horror and disbelief on Molly's face, Gran nodded at her, "oh yes this cottage has been in the family since the Doomsday book, or earlier. I'm sure it has many stories to tell that we may never know about. There have been some additions, but the foundations are the same."

Molly glanced again at Ghost Mary. Did she have my bedroom? No wonder she seems comfortable in this house. This is her home. Yet she must have been so frightened. Home is where you should feel safe. Nothing should be able to hurt you.

She remembered the time when children she thought were friends had come outside the house, teasing and mocking her for having no parents. She had been frightened then, but they didn't want to kill her. How horrible. Poor Mary. Molly couldn't believe she was actually feeling compassion for the Ghost. Mary had made her question her own sanity and here she was feeling sorry for her.

"What are you looking at Molly? Is there something there?"

"Erm, nothing Gran, I was just looking and wondering about the people who used to live here before we were born."

Molly didn't want to scare Gran with tales of Ghosts in the cottage. So she kept it to herself. She was sure she could solve this.

Gran looked doubtfully at Molly, "hmm, well to get on. Apparently, the mob found signs of witchcraft, everything explainable, but at the time, well it was different. They found curdled milk, a sure sign of a witch they thought. Mary had milked the cow so it was her to blame. Mary would always give an opinion and argue black was white if she thought she was right. Women didn't do that, another sign she was a witch." Gran sipped at the dregs of her tea. "Do you want another drink? I'm going to get more tea."

"Can I have hot chocolate?"

Gran smiled and went to the kitchen counter where she busied herself making tea and hot chocolate. Gran stopped talking for a moment while she gathered things together, but then she continued at the same time as Ghost Mary started to fill in some gaps.

So far she mostly got it right, but if Mother had been home that day things might have been different. She had gone up to Colhome Hall to attend the Marquis. He had a cold, of all things to be called away for. My sister took my brother and was gathering herbs in the woods. I was home alone preparing supper for when everyone came back. Father was at work, he was a carpenter and had a commission to repair a church. He'd been gone for months and we didn't know when he would be back.

Ghost Mary went silent. Molly could feel the sadness coming from her, she had faded back to a shadow.

"Are you listening, Molly? You've gone into a world of your own. I thought you wanted to know this?"

"Sorry Gran, yes I'm listening. I was just thinking," Molly lied.

Gran continued after casting a wary glance Molly's way. "It was a time when no woman was safe, if they were single and rich they were a witch, if they had a wart they were a witch, if they were female they were a witch. Poor young Mary was the scapegoat for everything that went wrong. The mob called her a witch and hung her from the big oak tree in the woods."

Gran had finished making the drinks and brought them over to the table.

Molly paled. That was what the Ghost had meant by a sad tree. It was the one she had been hung from. How awful for her to even see it again.

"You ok honey? You look a bit pale, here get some of this hot chocolate down you, that'll perk you right back up."

Gran watched while Molly took a sip of the hot drink, finishing with a cream moustache which she wiped away on the back of her hand.

"You realise why I couldn't tell you while Aisha was here? It's not something to tell everyone. Some people in the village, well they are ancestors of the ones that did this. If we want a peaceful life we don't cause trouble with accusations. Do you understand?"

Molly nodded and Gran continued.

"Such a terrible thing to happen right here in this cottage and I didn't want to frighten Aisha. Her parents can be the ones to tell her about Colhome's terrible history. It's possible that her ancestors were involved too."

Involved? They stood by and let it happen, made it happen. They need to pay.

Molly paled at the anger in Mary's voice. She couldn't see her, but the voice sounded so close Mary could be sat at her shoulder.

Taking a sip from the tea Gran waited a few minutes before she continued. She didn't notice Molly's discomfort, her eyes focused on the table. "Now the watch," said Gran as she lifted it off the table and turned it around in her hand. "It's obviously Mary's, but girls didn't normally have pocket watches. They wore watches around their necks like a pendant, if they were rich enough to own one. It's strange that Mary had one and an expensive one too. We've never been a rich family. Comfortable, but not rich."

"Maybe she had a rich friend? It would have to have been a male though," Molly said. Male and a betrayer she thought.

"Well, it would be frowned upon for a well-to-do boy to mix with a common girl and to give a gift such as this...if anyone found out there would be real trouble," Gran said. "Maybe the notebook will give us some clues. It could be another reason she was accused of witchcraft though, enchanting a rich boy."

After taking another sip of the aromatic tea Gran concluded, "anyway that's the story. Hiding it stops rumours. Even after all these years, rumours would still circulate. I think much of the tale has been lost over time or maybe even changed a bit to make it easier to tell, but that's the basics. If you want to read this notebook I would be happier if you kept it locked in the drawer when you're not reading it. It's very fragile and I wouldn't want it to be damaged."

You know it's private? It was hidden on purpose, so no one could see it. You don't have a right to look at it. It's mine!

Molly looked at the shadow in time to see her solidify and then wisp out again. It was obvious the Ghost wasn't happy that people would read her private thoughts, but she was dead. People read dead people's stuff all the time. It stops being private when you die. But Ghost Mary was still around to see what people thought, does that make it different?

"Thanks Gran, I'll be very careful with it and keep it locked in the drawer. I think there's a mystery to solve here and I intend to solve it."

"You mean about the pocket watch? Yes, that is a mystery."

Molly left the pocket watch on the table and after retrieving the notebook headed to her room. Laying on her bed, sunlight through the window providing welcome warmth, she opened the first page. Drawings of herbs, their names and uses met her eyes, garlic, sage, tarragon, all common herbs. She flicked through them.

Ergot, that was one she didn't know, she looked at the picture and its explanation.

A fungus growing on wheat and rye. Used in childbirth, stops bleeding. Too much causes St Anthony's Fire and death.

Could that be what happened to the woman and baby?

Molly looked around, but the Ghost was nowhere to be seen. She would ask Gran about it later. She continued through the pictures and explanations of different herbs until she found an entry about Mary herself.

I met a boy in the woods. Stupid boy had been playing with plants, his hands were blistered and swollen. Mother soon sorted him out though.

More pages of herbs followed then;

His name is James. He came back to see me, found me talking to myself. Who would believe the Marquis's son would be interested in me. We ran in the woods, laughed and talked. He seems nice.

"The Marquis's son? He would be rich. He could have given the pocket watch." Molly spoke aloud hoping the Ghost would confirm it for her, but all was silent.

A few more pages of herbs then the book became more a diary than a log of plants. Molly skimmed through looking for something to give a clue what happened.

James Darling, what a lovely name, it sounds more like an endearment than a name. He laughed the first time I said it.

Molly looked up from the book. "Darling, that's Aisha's surname. Could they be related? Surely not. Aisha would know if she was related to the rich and powerful."

A knock came on Molly's door and Gran came in, "talking to yourself again?"

Molly laughed, "the only way to get good answers Gran."

"Hmm maybe, anyway it's time you were asleep young lady. I'll take the book and lock it up, you get yourself some rest."

"Ok Gran, see you in the morning, good night."

Gran took the book and left Molly to get ready for bed.

"Wish I could have read a bit more, but tomorrow's a new day. Wonder if I can catch Aisha before she leaves in the morning, ask her about this James person."

They hang you as a witch for that you know, that's what they said about me, talking to the Devil they call it.

Chapter 6

The next morning was miserable, rain poured and thunder cracked. Molly was glad she didn't have to do anything except read the notebook.

Gran had gone out early, Colhome Hall was no longer the seat of the rich and powerful landlord, but a museum. Gran worked there three days a week. Today was one of those days. When Molly had been younger she would wander the Hall or help with filling shelves while Gran worked, but she was old enough to look after herself for a while now. Gran always left a pot with stew or some such stuff for her lunch.

"First thing first, phone Aisha."

She headed downstairs still in her pyjamas, poured milk on cereal and orange juice in a glass, placed them on the table then grabbed the house phone. She dialled the number for the Marquis Arms and waited, hoping Aisha was still home.

"Hello Marquis Arms, how may I help you?"

"Mrs Darling is Aisha still there?"

"Sorry Molly, she left at six this morning. You could try her on her mobile, or send her a text and when she has a signal she can ring you."

"Ok, thanks."

Molly was gutted, she had no one but herself to talk to.

"Where did I put my mobile?" She downed her juice while she considered, then started on the cereal. "Last time I used it I was in my room, it must be upstairs."

Leaving the half-eaten cereal and a dirty glass on the table she dashed upstairs. "Yikes this room is a mess, how am I going to find it?" Picking up her dirty jeans she shook them, nothing. A chair in the corner was full of clean clothes she hadn't thought to put away. Stuffed animals peeked out between the clean underwear. "I suppose if I tidy up in here I might have a better chance of finding it."

She set to, putting away clean clothes, and throwing dirty ones in the wash basket. Books back on bookshelves. Shoes and trainers into the bottom of her wardrobe. Schoolbag onto the top of the wardrobe.

"Oh, I wonder..." Molly opened the school bag and sure enough, there was her mobile. Seven missed calls and loads of text messages. She scanned them quickly, nothing important she would deal with them later. Mostly they were from girls at school who were never really nice to her. Answering their text would be like putting her head in a snake pit and hoping it only contained a grass snake. The battery was just about dead so she ran back downstairs to plug it in. At least the charger was always in the same place. Gran saw to that.

She typed in the text to Aisha asking her to ring asap. Then sat and looked at the phone, hoping it would ring straight away. It didn't.

She set to doing chores, washing pots, making her bed and sweeping up. Then she sat and waited for the phone to ring. Tapping her fingers on the table didn't cause it to ring. She checked it was charging properly and the sound was on then wandered around the cottage three times, before deciding to read more of the notebook. After unlocking the drawer she withdrew the book and sat on the sofa, feet curled under her and hunted for the page she had got to.

He comes to see me most days now. We found a den inside an old oak tree where we can sit and talk. He brought some conkers threaded with string and we bashed those together for ages. His broke first. I won!

More pages of herbs, then a list of potions and what or who they were for.

Flax seeds – to stop swelling, cleans the blood.

Lavender – to ease anxiety.

Policeman Lewis – needs Ginger for his wife who is with child.

Ann Butcher, broke her arm, flax seeds for pain.

Mrs Smith – Raspberry leaf tea to ease birth.

Molly skipped through even more until she found more diary entries.

He promised we would be friends forever, together forever. He brought me a watch, a man's watch. He had it inscribed for me. I hugged him tight, I never had such a friend, actually, he is my first friend. Everyone always wants something from me. They think I am weird, but they happily use my skills.

Tring tring, tring tring.

Molly jumped, almost dropping the book. She'd been so lost in the notebook she forgot about the phone. Grabbing it from the table she checked who it was.

"Aisha, at last."

"Hi Molly, we just got here. I haven't had a signal nearly all the way, it was so boring. Wassup?"

Molly spent the next 30 minutes telling Aisha the story of Ghost Mary. No matter what Gran thought, it was important that Aisha understood what the Ghost was about. Then she continued to tell her what she had read and asked if she knew anything about James Darling.

"Well I've never heard it mentioned, but I'll talk to Nan, she may know. I'll check Google too. I'll ring you back when I have news. How's Ghost Mary? Is she still annoying you?"

"Actually I haven't seen or heard her all morning. She's been unusually quiet."

"Well let's hope she stays that way, for your sanity's sake. I need to go now Molly, have to unpack and Nan needs hugs and stuff, you know how these wrinklies get. Love her to pieces, but she squeezes a bit too hard."

"Ok Aisha, talk later, have fun." Molly put down the phone and looked around, where was the Ghost? She was very quiet.

Taking advantage of being alone for a while she decided to look for the den in the tree. The rain had stopped and the sun was poking its head through the clouds. First putting away the notebook, she slipped into jeans and t-shirt, socks and trainers, then after locking up the cottage she headed to the woods.

She loved the smell of the woods after the rain, the sweetness from the damp earth, and the water and oil combination from leaves, the whole musk smell made her feel alive. She spun around wheeling her arms. Drips from the leaves wet her bare arms bringing her back to the mission.

"Now an oak tree it said," Molly mused aloud. "There was the one the Ghost said was sad. We thought it was the one she was hung from, but just maybe…"

Molly headed in what she thought was the direction of the oak tree, but she soon found herself lost. She'd never been lost in the woods before, she'd grown up running through them, "how can I be lost?"

She heard the snicker before she saw the shadow. Then it dawned on her, the oak tree was in a sunlit glade, surrounded by grass and wildflowers. The Ghost was doing something to her, making her see shadow and darkness, leading her astray. Mary was playing with her. She'd thought her gone, but she was watching. Each time Molly would head in the right direction Mary forced her in another.

"Leave me alone, how can I help you find peace if you don't let me try."

Peace? I can never find peace. I was betrayed by my one friend. The one I trusted with my life and it was taken from me, because of him!

Molly looked for Mary, but she was nowhere to be seen, even the shadow had disappeared. Leaning against an elm tree Molly stopped and considered. She would have to stop saying her plans out loud because she realised, Ghost Mary was not going to let her go to the tree. She couldn't let Mary know what she was doing. And if she ever wanted peace from the Ghost she would have to learn why James Darling betrayed her.

As she stood there watching streaks of sunlight weaving their way through the leaves, reflecting from droplets of rain and dazzling her eyes she saw a young couple heading towards her. Laughter spilt from their lips as they ran carrying a basket covered in gingham cloth between them. Molly called to them, "damp day for a pic...nic." They vanished. Molly looked around, where did they go? The only sound was the creaking of trees and water dripping from leaves as they rustled in the breeze.

"Ok, this is really not funny." First a Ghost and now, could she be having visions? Normal girls do not have visions or see Ghosts. Maybe she was going crazy. Maybe none of it was real. "No. Mr Lewis saw the shadow. I'm not crazy."

Crazy Molly. That's what they called me, that's what they'll call you.

"Go away, leave me alone. If you don't want my help then what do you want?"

Molly didn't get an answer. Not a vision, not a shadow, nothing.

She had a choice, try again to find the tree or go eat lunch. It was getting quite late and Gran would be home soon. She wouldn't be happy if Molly hadn't eaten, so taking a deep breath to steady herself, she chose to go home and eat. She would search for the oak tree after lunch, but this time she wouldn't say it out loud.

After placing the shepherd's pie in the oven to warm she went to the edge of the woods with a bag. She'd spotted some feverfew and knew Gran was running short. A quick gathering would put Gran in a good mood when she got home and give Molly something to do while she waited for her lunch.

She looked around for other herbs as she gathered, she

hadn't brought gloves so the young nettles would have to wait, but she noticed a bunch of wild garlic, she could take those too. Heading into the woods slightly, she could see the direction to the oak tree. Keeping her mouth firmly closed she headed in. She didn't want to give the Ghost even a hint of what she was up to.

Pretending to look for more herbs Molly slowly got closer to the old oak tree, keeping the direction firmly in her head she got closer and closer.

She knew when the Ghost became aware of her plan, she felt the push away, but she resisted. The more the Ghost pushed her away, the more Molly pushed forward until at last, there it was.

You shouldn't be here. Go away!

Ghost Mary screeched at Molly, but Molly ignored her. She wouldn't find anything out if she took notice of an angry Ghost.

The oak tree was huge, easily ten arm spans for Molly to reach around, fissures and knots distorted the dark bark. Red oak Molly thought, "I wonder how old it is? Probably planted at the same time as the cottage was built."

She walked around it slowly, looking for a hidden nook or anything that would denote a den to her. After she'd covered the whole circumference the only thing she'd found was a slit, quite narrow and even as slender as she was, she would need to breathe in to get through it. She would also need a torch. "How did you see in there?" she asked of the Ghost. Not really expecting an answer, she was surprised when she got one.

James had a covered lamp.

"Well, that explains that. Probably what I can smell burning. Oh no, the pie!"

Running as if all the Ghosts in the woods were after her Molly raced back to the cottage, pushing through brambles and gorse bushes, to take the shortest path. Covered in scratches she opened the door. Acrid black smoke poured out. Covering her mouth with her hand she ran in and quickly turned off the oven and opened its door. Her pie was a charcoal mess. The whole cottage reeked of smoke. "So much for pleasing Gran and having her in a good mood. She'll go six shades of purple when she gets back and smells this."

Serves you right for sticking your nose where I told you it wasn't wanted.

Opening the front as well as the back door, caused a draft which helped ease some of the smoke out. The rest she wafted out with a tea towel. The charcoal pie was thrown in the bin and the dish was put to soak. Molly wondered if it would ever come clean again. Once she'd cleaned everything away she took some ham from the fridge and made a sandwich which she ate slowly. A heavy feeling in her stomach made her appetite almost none existent.

She was worried, "Gran will be home shortly and this place fair reeks of smoke. What to do?"

Leaving the half-eaten sandwich on the table she headed into the pantry. A box in the corner looked promising. After dragging it out and opening it up she found bunches of lavender. Giving them a shake first to release some of the powerful scent, she hung them around the room. Even then the smoke was still quite potent, but it was the best she could do. After finishing her sandwich with a little more gusto, she took the diary out of the drawer planning to read some more. The phone rang.

"Hello?"

"Is my... Mrs Barber there please?" a woman's voice asked.

"Sorry, she's at work, can I help? I'm her granddaughter."

"I...I ...Molly...err, no it's ok I'll ring later."

The phone went dead. Molly looked at the receiver, "how strange."

You think that's strange? You don't know the half of it yet.

"What do you mean?

There was no answer.

"You know who that was, don't you? Why don't you tell me? You interrupt when it suits you, well now it suits me. Tell me!"

The Ghost wasn't talking.

Molly had just picked the notebook up again when Gran walked through the door. Putting the notebook back in the drawer with bated breath, Molly waited for the explosion when Gran got the scent of smoke. She was not disappointed.

Using the gathering of herbs as an excuse for the burnt pie, placated Gran a bit, but she found herself grounded anyway. Grounded until she'd prepared all the plants she'd gathered, as well as the ones Gran had in storage already. Made them into their various potions, then she could go out again. To deliver them.

Molly tried arguing, pleading and begging. Nothing worked, she was grounded for a week.

"The whole cottage could have burnt to the ground. A week's grounding is slim in comparison, consider yourself lucky."

Knowing Gran needed time to herself, just to calm down, Molly took the notebook and headed upstairs. Halfway up she remembered, "oh, there was a phone call for you, some strange lady. She put the phone down before I could find out who it was. Said she would call later."

Molly didn't notice the look of hope on Gran's face as she flopped into a seat. "Thanks," Gran said.

Molly was gone, up the stairs, too upset at being grounded to notice anything.

Chapter 7

ook Raspberry leaf to Mrs Smith. Advised her to make it into tea. She holds her swollen belly protectively. Her skin is very red, Mum will know, but I think she is ill, maybe from St. Anthony's Fire. I noticed rye in a sack.

St. Anthony's Fire?

Leaving the book on her bed Molly ran downstairs. "Gran?" she called.

Gran was still sitting on the sofa, a photo album in her hands. She closed it as Molly appeared and looked up, "yes?"

"What's St. Anthony's Fire?"

"What a strange question. We don't see it nowadays, why do you want to know?"

"It's mentioned in the notebook."

"Ah. It's poisoning from the fungus Ergot. Ergot grows on wheat and rye. It was common in the 1600s. If they had a bad harvest the price of wheat would be very high and the poorest people would gather rye instead of buying wheat from the farmer. If they weren't careful the rye could be covered with Ergot. Small doses are good for starting labour, but large doses kill. The poisoning is called St. Anthony's Fire, the skin becomes very red."

"If a pregnant lady had it and then was given something by Mary, people would think Mary did something?"

"That's entirely possible. People were very suspicious. It would explain how a woman and her child died and Mary was blamed."

Your Gran is wise, you should take more notice of her. My sister would be proud to see her.

Molly looked up in surprise. The Ghost stood close, a lovely smile spread across her face. It was the first time Molly had seen her smile or heard the Ghost say anything nice.

The Ghost wasn't just an ancestor, she truly was a relative, Aunt to both Gran and Molly. A very distant Aunt, but one all the same. Seeing the look of pride on Mary's face changed Molly's attitude. She didn't just want to help her because she was annoying and then would go away. She wanted to help because Mary was sad, angry and feeling betrayed. No relative should feel that way, not if Molly could help it.

Somehow James had betrayed her, but Molly was sure he couldn't have done it on purpose. The one who'd had the watch inscribed treasured the friendship. There had to be more to it. Something Mary didn't know. Molly decided there and then, she needed to get out of the house to investigate and to do that she needed to prepare the herbs. That would take a day, but then she would be able to go out to deliver everything. She needed to leave the notebook a while and set to work.

"Is that your mobile ringing Molly?"

"What? Oh yes. Sorry I was lost in thought."

Molly ran upstairs and reached her phone just as it stopped ringing. A quick check showed it was Aisha and she quickly returned the call.

"Hey Molly, do I have news for you."

"What? Is James a relative?"

"Nan thinks so. Hang on, I wrote it down so I wouldn't forget anything."

The phone was quiet for a minute with just the rustle of papers in the background then Aisha started to speak again.

"Nan's been looking at the family tree, can you believe it? Anyway, she says there was a James born in 1629 the son of the Marquis of Colhome. Apparently, we used to be quite the wealthy family in days gone by, my family lived at Colhome Hall. How's that for rich? All the money was lost in some shipping tragedy in the 1700s. Anyway, back to James, he had two older brothers Laurence and Caleb. They were both older than him by a lot, Laurence was born in 1620 and Caleb in 1624. The chances are that James would be lonely, especially if he lived in that huge hall with just his parents."

"Aisha get on with it."

"Sorry, was just thinking out loud, but Nan said that too. Can you imagine that huge hall and just you? No wonder he wanted a friend. Nan said it wasn't done in those days for the rich to mix with the poor. Especially a girl. Folks would say she bewitched him. After his money and all that."

"Aisha, what happened to James?"

"Oh yeh, well he lived to a ripe old age of 80 something, died in 1713. It doesn't look like he ever married though. Nan was looking more into him, he joined the church and went off to Africa as a missionary or something. She doesn't know yet if he came back home, she hasn't got that far."

"Does your Nan know anything about Mary? Anything she has that mentions her?"

"Not yet, but she has some old papers and I'll help her go through them, if we find anything I'll let you know."

"Thanks, Aisha, you're a real friend."

"So anything happening over there besides your Ghostly friend?"

Molly spent the next 20 minutes telling Aisha about the grounding, and everything leading up to it.

"Ow that really sucks, but don't forget to take a torch when you do go out. You might get a chance to look in the oak tree."

"You're right, I'll get one out and stick it in my jacket pocket. I think I'll do that now, then sort out all the herbs and stuff, with luck I'll get out of here for an hour tomorrow."

"Ok Molly, will chat when I know more. I'll go look through some more papers… boring."

"Thanks again Aisha, bye for now."

After putting down the phone, Molly grabbed the torch off her dresser. Downstairs she slotted it into her jacket pocket before entering the pantry and pulling out all the herbs and plants she could find. The book at the back of the pantry door held all the recipes. She took the book, placed it on the kitchen counter and set to work. The smell of herbs filled the cottage. The more she chopped and ground the better the smell. Molly loved it.

She'd just finished the healing poultices when Ghost Mary appeared, perched on the edge of the kitchen counter, watching

Molly work.

You're quite skilled you know. Those poultices, they have many ingredients I do not know.

Glancing to see if Gran was listening, she realised she was alone. Gran must have gone out, probably in the garden. That often happened when Molly was engrossed in potion or poultice making.

"There are many new plants from across the world that you may not know of," she told Mary. "Some Gran grows in the garden or greenhouse. Others have seeded here with all the visitors from abroad. Then there are the ones that are imported and Gran gets from the market."

It felt strange to be talking with Ghost Mary, she knew she must be careful, but if the Ghost would tell her more it could be useful.

"Would you tell me what happened?"

Molly looked up, but the Ghost was gone. The easy solution it would not be. She was going to have to find out for herself.

She moved from making poultices to making potions, pain-relieving ones, anxiety-relieving ones, and even ones for stopping someone from feeling tired after a poor night's sleep. The amount of each plant had to be just right or they could turn into poison potions.

Each bottle had to be labelled with the name of the potion and the date it was made. Molly worked carefully and deliberately. She didn't notice Gran had returned until the phone rang.

"Molly, go to your room while I take this call please, in fact, it's late so you may as well get ready for bed, I will clean up for you."

She quickly rinsed her hands and wiped them on a towel, then headed upstairs. At the top, she stopped to listen. Who could Gran be talking to that she didn't want Molly to hear?

"It's good to hear your voice."

"Yes, she's fine."

"No, nothing yet. I thought maybe yesterday, but then nothing happened."

"Yes, I know, it was the same with you. You were older though, so there's time."

"She fainted after a cut. Then I thought the signs would show. Maybe she doesn't have it. It has been known to miss a generation, rarely, but it has happened."

"No, no she's fine. Wood in her hand, but a poultice soon had it fixed. Plus a little extra while she was unconscious. She didn't see, don't worry."

"When will they let you out? You sound so much better. More rational. She has started to ask more questions and she found some stuff under the floorboards. If it was going to show I think then would have been the time, but nothing."

"Ok love. Call me when you can. I'll keep my fingers crossed that you're home soon. So glad you're feeling better."

Molly tip-toed to her room, avoiding the creaking floorboards. What hadn't she seen? What would show? Coming home? Gran had a brother in Canada somewhere, but it was definitely a female who called. Could it have been her Mum? A glimmer of hope lit up Molly's stomach. Could her Mum be coming home at last? For almost 8 years she had been gone, disappearing on the same day her Dad had a fatal car accident. Gran had always been evasive about it, just saying it was grown-up stuff. "This cottage is full of mystery and questions. I need answers."

Molly was tired and fed up. Her fingers were green and sore from the plants and she felt alone. The only person to talk to was Gran and she was keeping secrets of her own. She knew if she told Gran about Mary, Gran would say she was 'away with the fairies.' She couldn't see Gran understanding what was happening any more than she did.

What do you want answers to?

The Ghost had been so quiet Molly almost forgot about her constant presence, but she was actually one of the answers she wanted. "Why are you here? Why can I see you? That would be a good place to start."

Those are easy questions, I'm here because every year just before the week of my death I come back to try to change what happened. As you can see I'm not successful, I'm still here.

You can see me because it's in your blood. Literally. You spilt your blood on me. I may not be a witch, but I do know that spilt blood is powerful. You should be more careful.

Molly stared in surprise. "You mean it? It's my fault I can see you and you're here every year since well …." Molly looked to the ceiling as she tried to do the maths. "Almost 400 years. That would be 400 tries to fix it and you can't? No that's not right. More like 350 years, but still that is one heck of a lot of tries. Maybe I can help you?"

I doubt it. Unless you really are a witch. Do you have magical powers?

At Molly's crestfallen look Mary snorted.

Didn't think so.

"Well if you stop blocking me when I try to investigate, you never know what I might find out that could help you. At least you have to let me try. Aisha's doing some research, she could find something out."

Aisha, pfft. Just another Darling to betray us. Don't expect help there. They pretend to be nice, then when your back's turned they stick in the knife. Lead you to your doom.

The Ghost vanished and Molly was left alone in her room. Lying on her bed, arms behind her head, she thought about what the Ghost had confirmed for her. James Darling had betrayed her. But had he done it knowingly and to what end? It didn't make sense.

She had no idea how she was going to fix the past, but she felt in her bones that the tree was the best place to start. She needed to get out of the cottage. Tomorrow she could take some of the stuff she'd made to people in the village. Gran would let her do that. If she came back through the woods a small diversion to the oak tree wouldn't be noticed. Molly was sure there was something there to give a clue about what to do next.

Chapter 8

The next morning Molly rose early to finish the rest of the potions. If she wanted to get out she needed to be prepared. She'd checked the torch was still in her jacket pocket ready. She just needed to finish making everything. She was mixing the final potion when Gran appeared, dressed and ready to go out.

"Old Mrs Cluck's neighbour phoned last night, she had a fall and needs a visit this morning, so I'll take the potions into town with me," Gran said. "You need to stay here. There's a herb and spice delivery today so someone has to stay to receive it." With eyebrows raised, she added, "try not to set the house on fire today."

Molly only had time to say, "but Gran," before she'd picked up the bag of prepared poultice and potions and was gone out of the door.

"Damn, how am I supposed to investigate now? Aargh, I would scream if I thought it would do any good." Molly stamped around the room, picked a cushion up and threw it back down again. Opened a cupboard door and slammed it shut. Stamped up the stairs and then stopped, wondering what to throw her frustration at next. "Guess I'm stuck here, again," she said as the realisation hit her. There was nothing more she could do.

You really should stop talking to yourself you know.

"Why? It's the only way to get sensible answers." Molly knew that was total rubbish, but the last thing she wanted was a ghost telling her what to do. She had enough with Gran bossing her around.

She couldn't even sneak out while Gran was gone if there was a parcel coming. This was not how she'd planned to spend the summer holidays. Nothing was going to plan. She was almost 16 years of age and she was grounded. A part of her wanted to defy Gran and go out anyway, but she knew if the parcel arrived and she wasn't there she would be in even more trouble.

Molly tidied and cleaned the kitchen counter, put away all her equipment and hung the book back on the pantry door. She tried watching TV, but there was nothing she wanted to watch. She picked up the notebook and put it down again. She didn't want to know any more at the moment. She wanted to get to the oak tree and see what was inside. She could think of nothing else. If only the parcel would arrive quickly, then she might have time to get out and back before Gran returned.

She peered through the window, but all she could see was the village green, a couple of people walking, too far away to tell who it was. Nothing else. She sat down on the sofa, twiddling her hair wondering what she could do while she waited, but after a couple of minutes, she heard something outside. She ran to the window, then stopped, "what?"

Outside the window, there were woods, no village green. It was dusk. A tall blonde-haired boy was standing at the door with a girl. "Tha...that's me," Molly said, "but it can't be.

Where's the village green? The houses on the other side? How can it be getting dark?

Molly ran to the door and yanked it open. The sun blazed through the door into the cottage, there was no one there and the village green was where it had always been.

"I really am going crazy."

Sliding to the floor with her back against the open door Molly began to shake. Her whole body shook, she was frightened and alone and strange things were happening around her.

"Calm yourself girl. Deep breaths."

What was happening to her? She was seeing things that weren't there. She had a Ghost haunting her and Aisha was miles away at her Nan's in Scotland. She had no one to confide in. She had to work this out herself.

"I am not crazy. I am not crazy."

Talk to yourself like that and folks will think you are.

"Go away. Leave me alone."

"Hey, miss. Are you ok?"

Molly looked up to see a man with a parcel in his arms, how long had she been sitting here? She'd not seen the delivery van arrive. She hadn't heard him come through the gate and now he stood looking down on a trembling wreck of a girl. Pulling herself together as quick as she could, she stood up, "Yes, yes I'm fine thanks." She decided against trying to explain, he would think her 'loop the loop' if she did.

"Ok, if you're sure. I have a parcel for Mrs Barber," he said.

"Thanks, I'll take it."

Molly took the parcel to the kitchen counter and left it there. Her arms still trembled, but the shaking had stopped. A glance at the clock showed Gran had been gone an hour. She could be back any time, depending on how bad Mrs Cluck was and what Gran needed to do for her.

Gran wasn't a nurse or a doctor, but she was amazing when it came to helping sick folks. The hospital was two bus rides away and the local GP didn't like to do house calls, so the villagers always called Gran when they needed help. They usually paid with food, most folks didn't have much money, but Gran would have gone for free if it meant she helped someone.

As Molly thought about this she realised that maybe Gran could help her.

"If I really am two sandwiches short of a picnic, Gran will know and help me I'm sure. Maybe I need to see a doctor."

What do you mean?

Turning around Molly saw the Ghost sitting on the sofa watching her. "It's a saying, means I'm going crazy, mentally unstable, round the twist, I have a mental health problem."

Hahaha, that's funny, two sandwiches short of a picnic. I don't think you are though. I think it's the family thing.

Molly was about to ask 'what family thing,' but once again the Ghost was gone.

"Why does she do that? I never get any straight answers from her."

"Straight answers from who? And why was the door open?" Gran said as she closed the door firmly.

85

Ignoring the first question Molly answered the second saying that the box had just arrived and she hadn't gotten around to going back to close the door. "How's Mrs Cluck?"

Gran smiled, "she'll be fine, more shocked than injured, just a couple of bruises. A bit of arnica ointment soon had her sorted."

"Good, that's good. Think I'll read a bit more of the notebook if that's ok?"

"Actually Molly, no. I want you to help me move that old cabinet in the pantry. It's ancient and rotting, been in there since forever I think. I called the council to come and pick it up so we need to get it outside for collection."

"Really Gran? Do I look like a removal man?" Molly held up her arms to show the spider's kneecap muscles. "No way can I move that thing and you're not exactly muscle man either."

"Less sass from you missy or you'll be grounded longer."

Molly looked to the floor and bit her lip to stop the answer that almost flew out of her mouth. She didn't need grounding for longer. She had to get out sooner. Anyway, Gran would soon realise the two of them couldn't move it.

"Now come on, get some shoes on we don't want squashed toes. Then we'll see how strong you really are." Gran turned her back and headed to the pantry, the discussion was over.

Molly huffed and puffed loudly as she went to collect her shoes, muttering to herself that she really didn't need this after the morning she'd had.

Shut your whining, be grateful you have a Gran. Mine died before I was born. You can either move the thing or not, the least you can do is try.

Molly glanced at the Ghost, she looked like Molly looked when Aisha was being a brat. She couldn't help herself, she started to laugh. The Ghost was right, Molly was behaving badly. She was grateful to have Gran and she should help her, even if they found they couldn't do it.

Gran had heard the laughter and was soon shouting upstairs to Molly. "What are you laughing at? Come on we have work to do."

"Nothing Gran, just thinking. I'm coming."

Molly pushed and Gran pulled. Molly pulled and Gran pushed, but the cabinet wouldn't move. Gran tried to move it away from the wall, but got a torn nail for her troubles and nothing else.

"Ok cup of tea and thinking caps," Gran said as she wrapped a plaster around her torn nail.

Molly made the tea, Gran's finger looked painful and blood was seeping through the plaster. Blood in tea was not Molly's idea of a nice drink.

"There must be someone strong we know," Gran said as she flashed images of the villagers through her mind.

"There are workmen at the Marquis Arms, maybe a couple of them would come and help?" Molly suggested.

"Good idea Molly, I'll ring them to see if we can borrow a couple of lads."

They'd just finished drinking their tea when there was a knock and the front door opened. Mr Darling popped his head around, "cavalry here. What's this heavy thing that needs moving?"

Arrgh not another Darling in here. Get out!

Molly couldn't believe her eyes as Ghost Mary pushed Aisha's Dad back outside the door.

"Woops, sorry. I'm not normally so clumsy," he said as he caught the door handle, stopping himself from falling over.

Molly saw the look of distaste on Mary's face just before she faded from view.

Gran got up from her seat and showed Aisha's Dad into the pantry. He had two men with him that Molly hadn't seen before, she guessed them to be the workmen.

"Soon have that out of the way," he said. "Where do you want it?"

"On the pavement outside. The council will pick it up this afternoon," Gran replied.

Molly sat on the sofa out of the way, watching as the three men made short work of removing the cabinet that she and Gran couldn't move at all.

I told you, Darlings will betray you. You should keep them out.

Molly looked around for Ghost Mary, but she couldn't be seen. Just the voice of sadness and betrayal echoed in the room. Molly couldn't help feeling sorry for her, but Mr Darling wasn't to blame for what happened to Mary and Mary should stop blaming him and his family.

"Thank you," Gran said as the three men left. Then she beckoned Molly to come and look inside the now huge pantry.

Molly spun a circle as she looked around, it certainly was huge. So much more space.

"I thought we could have more shelves on the walls to keep prepared potions, rather than having to send them out immediately. What do you think?" Gran said.

"Yes, good idea. That way when someone needs something you don't have to start making it," Molly nodded.

The old cabinet had been so rotten that Gran hadn't been able to use it. Molly assumed it was the dampness of the pantry that had caused it, though she had never thought to ask.

"Would you sweep it out Molly while I get lunch going?"

Molly nodded and grabbed for the sweeping brush kept in the corner. Cobwebs, dust and actual soil were everywhere. "Wonder where the soil came from?" Molly muttered to herself as she set to. "Hey Gran there's an old rug down here, really yukky, what should I do with it?"

"Get some gloves on before you move it, then put it with the cabinet outside. The council can take it."

Molly grabbed the gloves from under the sink and lifted the mouldy rug slowly and carefully, then much faster as she spotted something shining. Bending to the floor she rolled the rug quickly out of the way to reveal a metal loop. Using a hand brush she swept the dirt from around it and with one finger lifted the loop, then with a quick jerk she pulled. She felt the floor beneath her shiver. Getting off her knees she crouched and looked around. The soil on the floor had moved to reveal what looked like a trap door and Molly was standing on it.

"Gran, come and see this," she yelled.

Gran appeared in seconds, "what...?" she started to ask, but shut her mouth as she saw the trap door. "Be careful Molly it could be very heavy and we don't know what's beneath it, there could be a long drop."

Standing to one side Molly pulled the loop, more dirt shifted, but the door didn't move.

"Wait I'll get some string, we can tie it around the loop and pull it together."

Gran went back to the kitchen and returned a minute later, a long piece of string in her hands. She fastened it around the loop and together she and Molly pulled. Slowly the hatch opened. With a foot, Molly moved the mouldy rug so it wedged between the floor and the underneath of the hatch door.

"We should be able to push it up now," Gran said. "That was quick thinking with the rug Molly, well done."

They peered down into blackness, a musty dank smell hit their nostrils. "Fetch the torch from the kitchen drawer Molly, let's see what we have here," Gran said. "Probably an old cellar, but it's strange that I never heard about it."

Don't do it, Molly. Don't go down there. Don't even look. Trouble comes that way. Only ever trouble.

Molly looked around, but Ghost Mary was gone. She was puzzled, how could trouble come from a cellar? Unless it wasn't a cellar? She soon found the torch and took it back to where Gran was waiting. Shining it through the hole, it revealed stone steps leading down.

"Why would it be covered over Gran? That seems most strange. Do you think it could be dangerous?" Thoughts of what Mary had said crashed around inside her head. Were they going to regret going down those steps?

"No idea, but someone must have had a reason. Let's investigate, but be careful, the steps must be very old, they might crumble on the edges, stay in the centre."

With Gran leading the way with the torch, they ventured towards the blackness. A metal bannister hugged the wall and they clung to it as they edged forward.

You shouldn't be down here. It's dangerous, go back. Lock the door again and keep it locked.

Molly looked around, but in the blackness, she could see nothing. She couldn't ask questions without Gran asking who she was talking to, so she stayed quiet. The Ghost obviously knew about this cellar. Molly wondered again why it had been closed up.

They reached the bottom and Gran shone the torch around. Old shelving tumbled and forgotten, bottles tippled over, some whole and on their sides, others smashed. Bits of cloth. An old table and chairs, decayed and rotting. A dead mouse in a corner. Spiders scurrying away from the light.

"Well it will be a good storage area, but I'll have to get some workmen in, to put in lights and make the steps safe. Good find Molly." Gran headed back towards the steps taking the torch with her.

"Can I look around a bit more Gran? I'll be careful?"

Gran nodded and passed Molly the torch. "Shine it on the steps for me, so I can see my way out."

After Gran had gone Molly looked around for Ghost Mary, but of course, she wasn't there. "She never gives me all the information. She gives me more questions than answers," Molly grumbled.

She started to move things around a bit so she could see more clearly what was there. Some large bottles looked salvageable, so Molly moved them to the bottom of the steps. The shelves were broken so she put them in a rubbish pile. The old table and chairs were near a wall at the far side of the cellar. Heading that way Molly thought it looked darker. She shone the torch directly at the wall, but only blackness came back to her.

She pushed away the table, rotten with age and damp, it crumbled under her fingers, but Molly took no notice. She was sure she was looking at a tunnel. Shining the torch again to the wall, she could see that the cellar went on. It was definitely a tunnel.

Don't go that way, stay away from it.

Molly looked around shining the torch in the direction she thought the voice had come from. Ghost Mary was frightened, she looked terrified.

"Ok, ok, I won't, not yet anyway. Lunch should be ready. Don't worry, what you remember is in the past, it can't hurt us now."

Molly took one last look at the tunnel before heading back up the stairs. She was right, lunch was just about ready, warm quiche and salad. She would rather have had chips, but Gran said this was healthier and Gran did the cooking. As they ate Molly told Gran about the tunnel.

"It probably leads to another cellar," Gran said. "If you go in, don't go more than a few yards, more than that the tunnel may be unstable, it could cave in. Just go far enough to see if there is another cellar beyond the first one." Gran looked at Molly for assurance.

"I promise," Molly said with a nod.

Chapter 9

After lunch, Molly ran upstairs to check her phone to be sure Aisha hadn't called. No missed calls and no messages. She sent a quick text to tell her about the secret cellar and the tunnel, then headed back downstairs.

"Do we have more torches Gran? Or something to help light the cellar up a bit more. It's awkward with just the one torch."

"Take a look in your Dad's old work shed Molly. He liked DIY, he might have something in there."

Molly had only been in there once since her Dad had died, but before that, she had been a regular visitor. She'd loved to sit on the workbench by his side and watch him work. She opened the door and memories flooded back. The bench under the window where he did his work. The shelves on the opposite wall with all his bits and pieces in. The scent of him, his bristles before he shaved, the calluses on his hands, his wonderful smile. A sense of sadness overtook her, she missed him so much.

She shook her head trying to clear the memories so she could concentrate on finding a light source, but they wouldn't go away. The memories went from a trickle to a flood, happy memories of a Dad that tickled her until she couldn't stop laughing, gave her shoulder rides and never complained at the constant questions. A Dad that told her bedtime stories and left the light on, even after Mum had said it should be off. Smiling to herself she recalled the Dad that she twisted around her little finger. She remembered the night there had been a power cut and her Dad had been working late in the shed. Even though it was past her bedtime he let her stay with him. He had used a large battery-powered lamp. She could picture it even now.

Closing her eyes Molly remembered where he kept it. Hopefully, the battery still worked. Reaching under the workbench she found it, stashed in a large box. It was big and cumbersome, but she pulled it out carefully and pressed the ON switch. Nothing happened.

"Damn, the batteries must have died."

Flipping the light over she found the casing for the batteries. "Screws! Wouldn't you know it, nothing simple."

A drawer in the workbench held different screwdrivers and after numerous attempts, she found the one that fit the screws. She soon had the casing open. "Empty? Gran must have done that. At least the batteries haven't leaked."

Leaving the lamp where it was she ran indoors, "do we have those big batteries for the lamp Gran? It needs batteries."

"Check the cabinet cupboard Molly, that's where I keep spare batteries," Gran replied. Her hands dripping with soapy dishwater she continued washing pots.

The cupboard was full of spare wrapping paper, cards, old handbags and odds and ends. Molly shuffled things around until she found a pile of batteries, of different sizes. At the bottom were the ones she wanted. She pulled them out and the contents of the cupboard fell out with them.

"Less haste more speed Molly," Gran said.

With a sigh, Molly replaced everything tidily so the door would close again, then headed back out to the lamp.

After inserting the batteries and screwing the cover back on, she turned the lamp over, took a breath and tried the ON switch. "Yes, it works!"

Carrying it in both arms she took it to the pantry and placed it on the top step of the cellar, facing outwards to give its light across the whole area. The cellar was a square, black and plain, water ran in rivulets down the walls giving an earthy smell and the air a cold, damp feel. The tunnel was immediately obvious. Molly grinned to herself, this was exciting. She wished Aisha could have been here to explore with her, but she would tell her about it when she rang.

Grabbing the torch from the kitchen she headed back down the cellar steps. Moving the old table and chairs well away Molly peered into the tunnel. The light of the torch in her hand didn't show the end. Recalling her promise not to go too far Molly trod carefully forward. There was a bend. As she rounded the bend she found the whole tunnel lit, candles spaced evenly in sconces on the walls. The floor looked well-trodden and hard-packed, the walls were dry and the damp smell was gone.

"What? How?"

She moved back around the corner and all was darkness again. Forward and the candles appeared.

"Someone must be using this tunnel, but that means, people have been coming below Gran's house, my house."

Molly clenched her fists in anger that people could be so

rude. Why would they want to anyway? There was nothing there, only old rotten furniture. Turning off the torch she tucked it in the back pocket of her jeans and followed the lighted tunnel as it wound its way up and down. Occasionally small empty rooms were obvious at the sides of the tunnel, but mostly there was just the tunnel. She was determined to find out where it went and put a stop to whoever was creeping around beneath her house.

After what seemed like forever, but she guessed was around half an hour, she came to a door. It looked immaculate and expensive. Hardwood with gold-coloured T-shaped hinges, all polished until it shone. She opened the door carefully. It didn't even squeak as she stuck her head through the gap and looked around before stepping out and gaping in amazement. She was in Colhome Hall.

She'd been there with Gran of course, but only to the visitor areas, the rest was cordoned off with red rope, strung between golden poles. Now she seemed to be behind the ropes, there was no sign of them.

"It must be the private area."

The furniture looked immaculate but antique. Sofas, tables and chairs, bureaus and cabinets were everywhere. The room was huge. The scent of beeswax was in the air, huge windows with long drapes covered the entire outside wall and a hardwood polished floor was beneath her feet. A carpet runner ran the centre of the room. The door behind her was just one of five, all identical spaced between a brocade papered wall, covered with portraits and paintings.

There was no one around and Molly took great delight in touching the items and spinning around imagining she lived there at the time when Ghost Mary lived. How fabulous this place must have been then. Full of life and activity. She knew she should go back and tell Gran what she'd found, she'd been gone ages and she was grounded, but she was having far too much fun.

Moving slowly and quietly she ventured further, looking for someone, anyone, just someone who knew about the tunnel and why it was lit. Gran certainly didn't know or she would have said something. Opening the door at the farthest end of the room Molly poked her head out. It was the entrance to the Hall. The front door was to her left, big and majestic. Molly remembered it. It was the start of the tour where the gift shop should be, only it wasn't there. A carpet lead up the central stairs and the red rope was missing.

"This isn't right."

Molly started to move quickly through the Hall, her breathing getting faster as a feeling of panic filled her.

"This is all wrong, where are the ropes? The pamphlets about the Hall's history? The gift shop?"

She ran upstairs, through the maze of corridors and rooms until she reached the servants' quarters, and then she stopped. Soap and towels were in the rooms, clothes strewn on chairs, old shoes under beds, closet doors left open, people were living here. Could it be the same people who used the tunnel? She needed to find them. Find out what was going on.

She moved more carefully now, keeping to the edge of the

corridors, peeking around open doors before she moved on. Her heart beat strong in her chest and she felt her palms become clammy. She tried to slow her breathing so she wouldn't be heard. She had no idea who these people were or what their intentions were, she could be in danger.

Eventually, she reached the kitchen, the door stood open and she could see an old range cooker. An oak table stood in the centre of the room and whitewash covered the walls. The smell of meat and pastries hit her nose. A matronly woman stood at the table kneading dough and shouting orders to someone out of sight. Molly was so confused she didn't know what to think.

Suddenly a young girl in servant clothes came through the door holding a tray of tea and biscuits.

"Yes cook," she said as she walked straight past Molly, seeming not to see her at all.

"Wait," Molly called to her, but she kept right on walking.

Molly had had enough of sneaking around. She was confused, more than a little scared, but most of all she hated rudeness and that girl had been very rude, besides which no one should be here. Pulling her t-shirt straight, putting her fingers through her hair to tidy it and standing as tall as she could she marched into the kitchen.

"Can someone tell me what's going on here," she demanded.

The kitchen was full of servants, boot-boys, footmen, butler, waiting staff and the cook. No one looked up, no one stopped what they were doing.

"Halloo," she said, but still no one took any notice. She walked around, but it was as if she were invisible. She waved her hand in front of the cook's face. Nothing. She sat on a stool at the table, but still she was ignored. A bowl of fruit sat in front of her. It was a while since lunch and she was hungry. Picking up a banana, she started to peel it. Suddenly the place was in an uproar. Screams shrilled in her ears as everyone fled the kitchen. Molly jumped off her seat in fright, "What happened?"

She looked around the empty kitchen there was nothing she could see that would cause someone to scream. Sitting back on the chair she shook her head as she slowly ate the banana and tossed the peel in a nearby bin. She ran pictures through her mind, what could have upset those people so much?

Footsteps sounded and she saw a young man, pop his head around the kitchen door. The same man she had seen in her vision at the door to her cottage. The vision that had caused her to collapse and shake. Then voices sounded again.

"Honestly Master James, the banana lifted itself up and started to unpeel. This place is haunted I tell you."

"Don't be daft Mrs Long, there are no such thing as Ghosts," said Master James.

Molly leapt off her seat again, they ran because of her? They really couldn't see her? She knew she wasn't dead, so she couldn't be a Ghost. It didn't make any sense. She glanced around the kitchen. Things here were working, not like in the Hall she visited with Gran, with a cold fireplace and even colder stoves. Everything here was being used, this was not a museum.

Then she watched the people hovering around the door,

frightened of entering the cosy kitchen. Their clothing was old fashioned, bodice and full skirts to their ankles on the women and men had breeches and waistcoats. Clothing from the time of Ghost Mary. And…is that? Master James? Could it be the James? She walked over to them, she was invisible, and no one reacted. She was the Ghost now. How could that be? Had she moved back through time? That had to be it, but how? It was why things seemed wrong. She was actually there when the Hall was being used as a home.

Fighting down her instinct to scream and become hysterical, she thought about it. The tunnel, it must have been lit back in Mary's day. That must be when I moved through time, but I felt nothing. This might not be such a bad thing. "Don't panic Molly. Just use it as a way of finding more things out. This could be better than looking in the oak tree. This could give me more answers. After that, I can panic about how to get home again."

Molly almost answered herself, but instead, she took a deep breath to keep herself calm.

"It must have been someone doing a prank," said Master James. "Now back to work and no more hysteria, please. Father would fire you all if he heard this commotion." James walked away, leaving the frightened staff to decide who would go into the kitchen first. Molly followed him.

James moved through the Hall with the assurance that only someone born of money and privilege could. Confidence in every stride. He was tall, broad-shouldered and blonde, like Aisha. As Molly assessed him, she could see the family resemblance between him and Aisha. There was no mistaking they were related.

She followed him to what she knew was the drawing-room. It was part of the tour in her world. A cosy room with sofas and coffee tables. A desk next to one wall had a scattering of papers with an ink well and quill on one corner. A man stood looking out of a window, but he turned as James entered.

"Well, what was all the fuss?" he said.

James grinned as he replied, "they're seeing Ghosts. There was nothing there."

The man nodded. "Peasants, they're so fanciful. Which reminds me…"

James drew his brows together and pursed his lips as if he knew what was coming.

"That peasant girl you took a fancy to, it's time you left her alone. Don't go giving her ideas. Have your fun by all means, but Father would have a fit if he ever found out that you see the same girl every day. She's so far beneath us. You know nothing can ever come of it."

Molly could tell James was angry. His face was red and his hands balled into fists. "You don't know her Lawrence. She's kind and funny. The way she talks to herself as if saying it aloud helps her understand things. The way she doesn't care what other people think. Her family helps those less able than them. They are lovely people. Mary is lovely. Even though they have little they share what they have with me when I'm there. That is true kindness."

Lawrence marched quickly over to James, so close he

stepped that not a hair would separate them. He peered down at him. Although James was tall, he was still growing, and Lawrence was much taller. "Kindness, bah! That girl will not get you ahead in court or help you fund the Hall. You have a position to maintain James. You cannot be mixing with peasants. That girl has you bewitched, end it now… or I will."

Molly watched with shock and distaste. She knew she didn't like Lawrence when she first saw him, with beady eyes, a pointy nose and a high forehead. His hair was in need of a wash, as was the rest of him, he smelled bad. Now her dislike was deep down. What a horrible man. Gran's saying came into her head, 'beauty is skin deep, ugliness goes right through to the bone.' Now she knew what Gran meant.

James didn't move, his hands balled so tight his knuckles turned white, but that was the only visible reaction. "There is nothing to end. We're friends, that's all." Turning his back on his brother he started to walk away, but Lawrence wasn't done.

"You need to concentrate on your studies, you'll be taking your place in society and business very soon. Leave this Mary or whatever her name is, alone. I mean it James or I'll take it to Father."

James turned swiftly, his face drained of colour. "You wouldn't? You couldn't? They would lose their home," James looked horrified. "Mary hasn't done anything wrong. I knew you had a cruel streak Lawrence, but to do that…you would put a baby out on the streets?" With moist eyes, James turned and ran out of the door.

Molly didn't follow him, she needed to think. James really

cared for Mary, she could see that. She doubted that he would have willingly betrayed her. It had to be something Lawrence did. She was glad she didn't have a sibling if Lawrence was an example of what they were like.

Lawrence retreated to a desk. Molly walked over to see what he was doing. He had a notebook in front of him and he was writing. Gran had always said it was rude to read over someone's shoulder, but Molly didn't think this situation was what she was thinking of when she said it. Molly started to read.

She has him bewitched, she makes potions, has she given him some?

She talks to herself, does the Devil answer?

She is a wild thing, doing her own thing, not what is expected or right.

Is she a witch?

He closed the notebook and put it in a drawer of the desk, rubbed his brow as if he had all the worries of the world on his shoulders, and then marched out of the room.

Molly was horrified. If someone saw what he had put there, Mary would be accused of witchcraft for sure. It was obviously Lawrence who had betrayed Mary, not James. James really cared for her, she could see that.

Opening the drawer Molly removed the notebook, turned to the page Lawrence had just written on and tore the page from the book. "No one will find it now," she said to herself as she shoved the offending page into her pocket.

She ventured back to the kitchen. Not worried about being seen she moved quickly and assured, but she was careful not to frighten the staff. She wanted to hear what the kitchen gossip was. That would be a good hint as to the feelings of the people.

She found a spot in a corner where she didn't think she would be in the way. She didn't want someone walking through her. That could be decidedly uncomfortable. Sitting on the floor she waited.

She listened as the cook complained about a serving girl and the footman complained about his apprentice. She watched as silver service was laid out on a tray and fresh rolls and tea were added.

The butler appeared requesting more preserves. "Master James is taking repast in his room," he said. "Poor lad is quite besotted with Miss Mary, but you know Master Lawrence, he has a cruel streak that one. I couldn't help but hear as he threatened him to leave Miss Mary alone or the Marquis would be making the whole family homeless. Them with a babe too."

"Aye, he's a rotten one that one," replied the cook. "Master Caleb was always a good peacemaker, but with him gone to the war and all. Well, it's above our station, but if you ask me." She raised her hand as the butler made to speak. "I know you didn't but I'll tell you anyway. There are worse things in life than marrying for love. Young Master James should be allowed to find a girl he loves. Not one that the family approves of. That Lawrence he will do harm to Miss Mary, you mark my words if he doesn't."

The butler looked uncomfortable, but he nodded at the cook. "Is the tray ready?"

An elderly man appeared at the back door, clutching a cap

in his hand as he stamped muddy boots against the door plinth shaking mud everywhere. "Oh dear, oh dear," he muttered shaking his head.

Cook and the butler turned as one. "What?" they asked.

"That there Lawrence, I seen him talking with some folks, in the garden. One of them was that Joshua Smith and you know he blames Miss Mary for his Lily dying. He just doesn't want to believe it be the 'fire' what killed her. Anyhow they were all sneaky and not in the open. So I got closer. Heard Miss Mary's name and Master James's too."

Molly listened with bated breath.

Reaching into his pocket the gardener took out a small flask and took a drink. "Sorry I needed that," he said as he stoppered the flask. "Mr Lawrence he mentioned witchcraft to them. I'm sorely 'fraid of what'll happen now."

Molly had heard enough. Now she was sure Lawrence was the betrayer, it was time to go home and talk to Ghost Mary.

Without fear that she would be seen as she headed back to the door of the passage, she skipped along. She could tell Mary the truth and she could be at peace. No betrayal from the love of her life.

The room with the door was empty. She pulled her torch out of her pocket so she had it ready when the lights went out, and then she set off down the corridor. She hoped Gran wasn't going to ground her even more for being gone so long. She wasn't worried that the tunnel would collapse, it was well used and maintained. "I wonder what they use it for? It goes all the way to the cottage. Maybe it's a smuggler's tunnel. Were my ancestors smugglers? Gran would have a fit."

As she came to the bend to the cellar she turned the torch on, but she didn't need it, the tunnel remained lit. As she approached the cellar she found it dry and brightly lit too. The table was against a wall with two chairs close by. Shelves on one wall were full of potions, pickles and boxes of fruit and vegetables. The scents from them were pleasant and reminded Molly of the Market in Sheffield, but this wasn't Sheffield and she wasn't in a market.

Molly stopped in her tracks. "Oh my God!" She didn't move, she couldn't. She felt frozen to the spot. The torch fell from her hand as her palms became damp from sweat as fear overtook her. "Don't panic Molly, come on pull yourself together girl." Turning she ran back down the tunnel, "ok let's try this again."

Holding her breath she turned the corner again, "please let it be dark. Please let it be dark." It wasn't.

She was stuck in the past. There was nowhere to run. She had no idea how to get back to Gran, how to get back to her own time. She sank to the dirt as the panic hit. She couldn't stop the sob that escaped her lips as she hit the ground with her fists, then she screamed, "noooo," before finally letting the tears fall until there were none left.

There was no one to hug her better, no one even knew she was there.

Chapter 10

Molly had no idea how long she sat in the dirt sobbing out her despair, but when she heard voices she realised she had to get her act together and figure out how to get home. Putting her hands to the floor to stand up she felt the torch beneath her fingers, she really needed to take that with her. Plastic and batteries weren't made in the 1600s.

With the torch back in her pocket, she waited to see who would appear. The voices were coming from the pantry. The trap door was open and Molly could see shadows moving above. Wiping the last traces of tears from her face with the bottom of her t-shirt, she headed for the stairs. Pristine white and solid, with a metal bannister on both sides they felt much safer than they did in the future.

As she drew level with the trap door she slowed. Carefully she stuck her head through the hole. The pantry door was open. Molly could see two girls and a woman holding a baby on her hip as it sucked a fist, probably teething. One girl she knew instantly was Mary, the other had to be her great, great and so many more greats, grandmother.

Reminding herself that they couldn't see her, she moved into the room. A stone floor beneath her feet, oak beams on the ceiling, whitewashed walls, the smell of wood burning in the hearth with a pot waiting on the side ready for boiling, everything reminded Molly she was stuck in the past. It was her home, but it wasn't, everything was different. The only furnishings were a solid wood table and stools in the centre of the room, a cabinet with cupboards and drawers against the far wall and a straw padded chair near the hearth. A scatter rug on the floor and thick curtains completed the ensemble. The stairs leading to the bedrooms were in the same place as the future cottage. The back door was missing. Just one door in and out.

The girls had their backs to the pantry door listening carefully to instructions from their Mother. "Lizzie you're in charge of Alex today. I have to head to the Hall with some items for Cook. Would you gather some nettles, we're very low. The gloves are on the back of the pantry door. Mary, Daisy cow needs milking, the eggs need gathering and if you find any feathers bring them in, I want them for a new chair cushion. And...don't forget to feed the animals while you are out there."

Mother watched as the two girls nodded, then handed over the baby to Lizzie before slipping a cloak over her dress and heading into the cellar. Molly moved quickly out of the way, she didn't want anyone to walk through her or would they bump into her? She had no idea, but safety seemed the best policy.

Molly understood then, the tunnel was a quick way between the cottage and the Hall. Probably had a lot more uses than that over the years, but that was what Mary and her family used it for.

Moving further into the room Molly could see that Lizzie was at least two maybe three years older than Mary, taller, with long black hair. A mop cap kept the hair away from her face. She smiled to herself as she considered that her grandmother was beautiful.

She moved further so she could see Mary. A solid alive Mary, not yet tarnished by hatred. The one that considered James a friend. It was still like looking in a mirror, but her emerald eyes shone and her face glowed and the smile on her face gave her small dimples on each cheek. She was happy.

Molly followed Mary as she left the cottage through the one door. The woods totally surrounded the cottage. Molly didn't know when they'd been cut back to make way for the village green and more houses, but the whole cottage looked different. Different woods was just the start. The cottage had a thatched roof, not slate. There was a barn at the end of a trail through the woods and the garden gate was none existent. Molly didn't recognise her home.

She followed Mary who skipped along, carefree and happy, she hummed a nonsense tune as she went. A Shire horse roamed the grass and Mary rubbed its neck as she passed. "James is coming to see me today Chestnut," she said. "I know he's beyond me, but he is so wonderful, I think I might be falling in love with him. I might make us a picnic, that would be nice, what do you think?"

The horse neighed a response which Molly understood to mean, a good idea. Then Mary was off again to the barn. A couple of buckets stood next to the barn door, Molly glanced at them, one was obviously for milking the other for cleaning. The smell of vinegar hit her nostrils. Mary wasn't really taking notice of what she was doing, her head full of James and seeing him later. She picked up the wrong bucket as she made her way to the cow's stall. Molly remembered Gran saying that Mary had been accused of curdling milk. That would do it, vinegar for cleaning would curdle the milk.

"No Mary stop," she called.

Mary stopped and looked around. Had she heard? Then Mary carried on walking to the stall.

"Wrong bucket Mary," she tried again.

"Who's there?" Mary looked behind her, then walking carefully around the barn she began looking for someone, anyone who could be talking to her. Finding no one she set off again to the stall.

There was only one thing left for Molly to do, she gave the bucket a big kick, knocking it clean out of Mary's hand. Remnants of vinegar splattered the stall and Mary, but went right through Molly. Truly invisible Molly thought to herself.

Mary gave a scream and ran like the Devil himself was after her, back inside the cottage, where she sat in a corner shaking and crying. Her eyes tight shut, she started to chant, "I won't talk to myself again, I will be good, whatever you are leave me alone," over and over again.

Molly couldn't help but feel sorry for her, she remembered how she felt the first time she had encountered Ghost Mary.

Lizzie chose that moment to return from nettle gathering with baby Alexander screaming on her hip. Mary quietened but didn't open her eyes, tears trickling down her cheeks.

"Nettles are painful, silly boy. Bet you won't touch those again in a hurry. Now come here let's get some dock leaves on those stings."

Placing the baby on the table in front of her she patiently started to rub the leaves over the stings. The baby stopped crying with just an occasional hic sob. It was then that Lizzie noticed Mary sat in the corner.

"Mary-mol, what are you doing? You're supposed to be milking Daisy," she said.

Mary looked up through red-rimmed eyes. "There was something or someone in the shed Lizzie. It knocked the bucket out of my hand."

At Lizzie's doubtful expression, Mary added, "Honestly Lizzie, I swear it's the truth. I thought I heard someone speaking, but there was no one there. I'm frightened Lizzie, will you come with me?"

Picking up the now quietened Alexander, Lizzie headed out to the barn. Glancing behind her she said, "come on then."

The two girls and baby headed to the barn with Molly following behind.

"See Lizzie, look the bucket is over the other side of the barn. That's where it was sent flying to."

Lizzie handed the baby to Mary and then headed over to pick up the bucket. "Well there's no one here now and …do you see, this is the cleaning bucket. You would have curdled the milk. Put your brain to work Mary-mol or we'll have no milk for Alex, or us for that matter.

Mary's face drained of colour. "I thought I heard someone say 'wrong bucket', but I thought I was imagining things."

"Well, it seems you have a guardian angel. Now get on and do your chores before Mother gets back, or you'll need more than a guardian angel to protect you." Lizzie retrieved Alex from Mary and walked out of the barn.

Mary looked warily about her as she grabbed the milking bucket and moved toward Daisy. Sitting on the milking stool she set to work, but her head was moving constantly, looking around for anything out of the ordinary.

Molly was surprised and pleased that Mary had actually heard her. She was tempted to tease Mary, play tricks on her and totally make her pay for the torment that Ghost Mary gave to her. She didn't though, as Gran said, "two wrongs don't make a right." It would be cruel and this Mary hadn't done any harm to Molly. She did need to get through to her though, make her hear what Molly tried to tell her.

Molly decided against talking to Mary while she was milking Daisy, she didn't want any accidents with the milk. It was obvious the family wasn't rich by any means. Molly thought the cottage looked decidedly poor, especially when she considered how luxurious the Hall was. Milk was probably part of a staple diet for them and an accident with it could be devastating. They could even use it to make cheese, cream or yoghurt and sell that for extra money.

When Mary had the milk stored safely away and was leading Daisy out into the woods where she could graze the small tufts of grass Molly thought it a good time to try talking to her again.

"Can you hear me Mary?"

Mary kept walking, leading Daisy out of the barn.

"Come on, I know you can hear me."

"I hear nothing, I hear nothing." Then Mary started to sing loudly, "tra la la, I hear nothing."

Molly followed until Mary had released Daisy and was turning around to go to the hen house and gather eggs.

"Stop right there Mary-mol," Molly said in the sternest voice she could muster.

Mary stopped.

"Good. Now find somewhere to sit, I know you can't see me, but we need to talk."

Mary fled. She ran as fast as her legs would take her, back into the cottage, up the stairs and hid behind a sackcloth curtain that divided the sleeping area. Her breath came in gasps and it took all her effort to calm down and stay as quiet as she could.

Molly sighed and followed Mary back to the cottage. She had no idea what to do. How was she supposed to stop Mary's death if Mary was too scared to listen?

Inside the cottage Lizzie was busy turning some of the nettles into hair conditioner by adding vinegar, others she set aside to dry out ready for use later. Alex was fastened to her back with a sheet and chomping on a hard stick.

Molly sat on the straw-padded chair by the hearth and stared into the flames of the fire. Her idea of helping Mary and so helping herself to get home was not going to work if Mary wouldn't listen to her.

"Mary where are the eggs?" Lizzie called upstairs.

There was no answer.

"I swear that girl is getting worse, what is she doing up there?"

"Laaybee," Alex pointed towards Molly.

"What're you saying Alex?"

"Laaybee, laaybee." The young Alex bounced in his sheet sling and grinned a three-tooth grin at Molly.

"There's no one there baby. Honestly between you and Mary-mol, I am not going to get anything done today."

Molly glanced up from the flames and found Alex staring directly at her. "You can see me? You can...you can see me. Yes! Ok, that's a start." Moving towards the baby Molly held out her hand, the baby reached for her and she did him a high five. His look of surprise turned to squeals of delight as he did it again and again.

"Unfortunately little man, you are not much help to me," Molly said. "Unless you can convince your sister that I am not some sort of Devil come to torment her."

Lizzie chose that moment to head upstairs and see what Mary was doing, passing straight through Molly. Molly didn't like that at all. It made her feel queasy and she wasn't sure if being sick was an option for her. She decided to keep well away from the people.

Alex called out "laaybee," but Lizzie kept walking. "What is that girl doing," she asked him, not expecting an answer.

Molly followed up the stairs. The door to Gran's room was open and a large bed and crib showed this must be the room Alex shared with his Mother. The bathroom was missing. They headed to Molly's room. The future bathroom had obviously been taken from here. Much larger than Molly's room in the future and divided with two pallets, one on either side of a sackcloth curtain. They found Mary still huddled behind the divider.

"What on Earth are you doing Mary?"

Mary didn't answer. She was still trembling with fear.

Lizzie pulled the sackcloth to one side, bent to her sister and put an arm around her. "Come on you, downstairs. A cup of camomile tea will have you sorted, then you can tell me all about it." After adjusting Alex to make sure the sheet supporting him didn't slip, she led her sister downstairs.

Molly stayed silent, although she found the idea of Mary and Lizzie drinking the same tea she drank with Gran as amusing, she stifled her laughter. She really didn't want to frighten Mary anymore. As she watched the two sisters, she realised she didn't know how long she had until Mary was accused of being a witch. How long until Lizzie and Alex lost their sister to mob rule? She wished she had read more of the notebook, but then again she didn't know the date now, where in time was she? She knew that Lawrence had started the ball rolling towards the final moments of Mary's life and she had to stop it somehow.

"The voice spoke to me Lizzie, there was no one there, but the voice…" Mary started to tremble all over again.

"Laaybee," Alex mumbled through the stick that was firmly wedged between red gums. The two girls ignored him.

"You sure you weren't talking to yourself again and the Devil answered?" Lizzie said.

"No, honestly Lizzie, I try not to do that. Mother said the villagers were whispering about me. That it was dangerous, I do try, I promise."

Passing Mary her tea, Lizzie directed her to sit in the straw-stuffed chair. "Ok now tell me what the voice said that has you so frightened."

Mary sipped the hot tea before answering. "It said it wanted to talk to me."

"Is that it?" Lizzie furrowed her brow. "That's not so scary."

"A voice from nowhere saying they want to talk to you is not scary? How do I know it's not the Devil? All this time I was talking to myself, the villagers knew I was talking to the Devil and now the Devil is talking back. Lizzie, I'm so frightened, I don't want to talk to the Devil. What should I do?"

Lizzie leant on the chair back and considered. Molly watched, what would Lizzie decide? If she put two and two together would she work out that there was someone really there from what Alex had said and what Mary was saying?

"Mary-mol, was it a woman's voice or a man's? The Devil is supposed to be male."

"Oh! It was a girl, definitely a girl, not a woman and not a man. So maybe not the Devil?" Mary looked hopefully at Lizzie waiting for some reassurance.

"Alex was pointing and saying something, it could have been lady…maybe?" Lizzie said, her brow crinkled in thought.

Looking up in surprise Mary put down her cup. "Could there really be someone here, a Ghost maybe?"

"Well, I'm not sure, but Alex is definitely pointing to something. It does sound a bit farfetched though," Lizzie replied.

"Alex is there a lady here?" Mary's trembling voice asked.

Grinning his toothy grin he reached toward Molly, "laaybee."

Both girls sank to their knees, made the sign of the cross over their chests and started to pray, "Our Father Who Art In Heaven."

"Oh for goodness sake, get up!" Molly said. "Prayers aren't needed, yet."

Mary stopped, but Lizzie couldn't hear Molly and she continued to pray. Mary grabbed her arm and told her what Molly said.

Lizzie's bottom lip trembled as she stood up, but she was determined to show no weakness. "Who are you? Why are you here? What do you want from us?" She demanded. Looking where Alex pointed proved quite effective at appearing as if she was talking directly to Molly.

"Mary, you'll have to tell your sister what I say. And…I'm not sure you'll believe me, I don't believe me."

Mary looked doubtful, but with a tremble in her voice, she told Lizzie anyway.

"Tell us," said Mary as she levered herself up from the floor and collapsed again into the chair.

Mary appeared pale, but Lizzie was decidedly white and Molly knew she would have to be careful what she said. Lizzie looked about to collapse at any moment and with Alex in her arms that would not be a good thing to happen. She started by saying her name and that she was 15 years old. She carefully told them where she came from, thoughts of witches still strong in her head she didn't want them thinking she was a witch. She explained how she had found the tunnel and somehow ended up in the past. She didn't think it wise to say that Mary's Ghost was haunting her. She didn't want to scare them again so soon. Instead, she continued to tell of her journey through the tunnel and into the Hall.

She was careful not to tell them anything they wouldn't know if Molly hadn't told them. It wouldn't do for them to know too much, that road could lead to more disaster. If she caused Lizzie to be accused of witchcraft too, it could be the end of the family line right there. Molly wouldn't exist if Lizzie didn't survive this and that made Molly doubly cautious. What a conundrum that would be, if Lizzie died because of Molly then Molly wouldn't exist, but if Molly didn't exist then Lizzie wouldn't die. It made Molly's head hurt just to think about it, so she knew she would have to be especially careful.

She did tell them about Lawrence though, and how he thought Mary to be a witch who had cast a spell on James. Slipping in how James had stuck up for her seemed a good idea, so Mary didn't doubt his sincerity. She missed out the part where they may become homeless. That would do no one any good to tell and they shouldn't know about it anyway. Then she told them how she had come back down the tunnel and still been stuck in the past. She didn't know how to get back.

The two girls had moved to the stools around the table while Molly talked, shaking their heads in disbelief and wonderment as Molly went through her story. After Mary had finished relaying the tale to Lizzie the whole room was silent. Baby Alex had fallen asleep, his tiny fist stuffed in his mouth.

Lizzie was the first to break the silence. "You mean, where you come from the Hall is not lived in? It's a museum? How far in the future are you talking here? Do you live in this cottage? The cellar was hidden? I can't imagine why." Lizzie had so many questions, but she had to rely on Mary to get the answers.

Molly answered as best she could without giving away too much, but when she said over 350 years in the future, Mary's mouth dropped open. As she passed it on to Lizzie she did it slowly as though she was trying to process it. Lizzie on the other hand was all business and took the news better. A raised eyebrow was the only indication of surprise.

It was Mary who first made the connection that they were related. "Wait, if you live in this cottage and your family always lived here, that means…" She looked at Lizzie. "This is one of our grandchildren, it has to be. Oh Lizzie we have to help her."

"So whose grandchild are you? Mine or Mary-mol's, or," Lizzie glanced at the sleeping baby, "are you Alex's?"

Molly grinned, even though she knew they couldn't see her she looked directly at Lizzie, her great, great and so many more greats grandmother. "I am yours, Lizzie."

Lizzie beamed, then blushed and looked flustered for a moment.

"Ah," Mary grinned.

Lizzie's face turned beetroot as she stammered out, "I'm to be married in two weeks, David, he's a lovely man, he works with Father as a carpenter. I guess then he will be your

Grandfather."

A knock on the door and Lizzie and Mary seemed to forget that Molly couldn't be seen. Mary started to whisper, "how do we explain her?"

Lizzie looked worried, "I don't know."

Molly couldn't help but laugh, "you don't have to explain me, no one can see me, well except Alex. I don't even need to stay quiet, no one can hear me except you, Mary."

Mary shook her head, "silly moment. Of course, no one can see you." Then with a grin, "or hear you," she said as she headed to the door.

Molly watched through the window, it was the same thing she'd seen in her vision, Mary talking to James at the door, it was getting dark outside. Was it just that morning that she had been waiting for the delivery and seen this? It seemed so long ago.

"Mary, I don't want to stop you from talking to James, but you really should get those eggs and feathers and feed the animals," Molly said.

Grabbing James by the arm, she called to Lizzie what she was doing and set off to the hen house.

Molly didn't follow, she didn't want to be a gooseberry in that relationship and it felt too much like being nosy. She decided she'd put her nose into Mary's business too much already, this was something Mary could do quite well on her own.

Instead, she headed to the pantry, she was thirsty and went looking for something to drink, water would be good. No bottles of water or running taps here though. She couldn't find anything, but she did know where the old well used to be. Heading outside she heard a gasp from Lizzie as the door seemed to open and close itself.

"The well is near Dad's shed, but there's no shed here, everything is different, how will I find it?" As Molly headed around the back of the cottage she needn't have worried, the well was obvious, surrounded by stone, a bucket with a rope attached was on the floor at the side of it.

Molly threw the bucket into the well and pulled it back up with the rope. It was full of fresh water. It tasted wonderful. Wiping her mouth with the back of her hand she was just putting the bucket back on the floor when she heard voices in the woods. Glancing around she could see flaming torches, lots of flaming torches.

She wasted no time. Running back to the front of the house she shouted, "Mary, Mary." Listening, she thought she could hear Mary's voice in the opposite direction to the barn. She set off running, shouting all the time.

Following the sound she eventually found James and Mary picking up feathers, a basket of eggs on Mary's arm.

"Mary, quickly you must hide. There's a mob heading to the cottage. They will call you a witch. Hide Mary please."

Mary looked towards the cottage. The torchlight was obvious now. The sounds of voices could be heard over the stillness of the night. Totally ignoring everything Molly had said she didn't hide but headed straight for the cottage. James ran beside her.

They reached the edge of the woods just as the door to the cottage was opened by Mary's Mother. They couldn't tell what was being said, but that didn't stop James from charging in.

"What's going on here? Leave these women alone," he said.

"Witchcraft, that's what it be," said a scruffy-looking man at the front.

A chorus of, "aye," came next.

The scruffy man had obviously designated himself the leader. "It's not right, women on their own. They can't manage excepting by witchcraft. I'm betting if we look around we'll find curdled milk. That Mary, she killed me own wife and bairn, poisoned her she did."

More "ayes" met this statement.

Mary's face went pale when they said that. She would never mix the two buckets again, but poisoning someone is not what she did. She would never do that. She had only given her raspberry leaf, for tea.

James took charge. "You all know me. Do you really think the Marquis's son would mix with witches? They are not alone as you said. Mrs Barber has a husband, he provides money for them while he works away. You've all done that so you can feed your families."

The crowd started to draw away as what James said rang true, but the scruffy man wasn't finished. "What about her?" he said pointing to Mary. "Talking to the Devil all the time. Not natural that."

Everyone turned and looked at Mary. Mary hid behind

James, she was very frightened now. If only she'd listened to Molly and hid away.

Mary's mother was not having them pick on her youngest daughter. "Speaking thoughts aloud is NOT speaking to the Devil. My Mary is a good girl, now be off the lot of you, or the next time you're sick I won't be offering my services. You'll be left to die in your own spitefulness.

The crowd moved off, but the scruffy man took another stab at Mary before he left. "I am watching you little lady, you be sure I'll get ya."

Mother leaned against the door with a sigh as the lights of the mob disappeared back into the woods. Then remembering her manners she thanked James for his help.

"It was the least I could do Mrs Barber. I must be off now, supper will be ready."

"Use the tunnel James, it's much faster than walking through the woods and safer too on a night like this," she said with a small smile.

James thanked her and headed into the pantry and down into the cellar. Lizzie closed the pantry door after him.

Mary's mother turned to her daughter, "well Mary-mol, looks like Mr Smith really has it in for you. You need to stay away from him. He tried to blame you when his wife died. No matter how many times I told him it was St. Anthony's Fire, he never believed me. Promise me you'll be very careful. Any excuse will probably have him back here again." Putting her arm around Mary's shoulders she gave her a quick hug before taking her cloak off and hanging it in the pantry.

Alex had woken up with all the noise and was sucking a crust of bread as he rested on Lizzie's hip.

"Laaybee," he said, giving the biggest toothy grin of the day and reaching toward Molly.

"What's that my man?" Mother asked Alex as she took him from Lizzie.

"Laaybee," Alex repeated grinning in delight at the attention he was receiving.

"It's ok Mother, he's been saying that all day, must be a new word he learnt," Lizzie said. She didn't know why she didn't tell her mother about Molly, but it felt right to keep it quiet for the moment.

Mother took Alex from Lizzie and sat by the fire with him. Tickling under his chin she made him giggle before she asked again, "what do you see my man?"

Molly waved to him from behind the chair causing Alex to shout with glee, "laaybee."

Another high five and Alex sent out giggles that caused the whole family to start laughing.

"Girls, I think your brother sees something. Do you know what?" Mother asked once the laughter had calmed down.

Lizzie and Mary looked at each other, should they tell? Mary blushed. She never had been good at keeping secrets. Mother knew instantly something was amiss.

"Ok to the table everyone and take a seat, maybe it's time to tell you something that may help you make up your minds not to keep secrets."

Closing the cellar and pantry doors, checking through the

windows to make sure no one was lurking and pulling the curtains tight, Mother followed them to sit at the table. "There is something you need to know," she said.

Molly was standing near the fire, but she moved closer so she could hear too. Whatever her great, great and so many more greats Grandmother had to say she wanted to know.

"This must not leave this room, understand?" she looked at her children waiting to make sure they were mature enough to keep a secret. Lizzie and Mary glanced at each other. What about Molly? Molly was family so silently they agreed, she didn't count. They nodded so she began.

"You both know that I have a 'talent' for healing," she said. It wasn't a question but a statement and the girls nodded.

"What you don't realise is, I can actually heal people. Heal cuts and make bruises go away. I am not so good with broken bones, but I can start them healing themselves."

Mary's mouth dropped open and her eyes widened with surprise, but Lizzie paled and looked at the table.

Mother looked pointedly at Lizzie, "you have something to say, Lizzie?"

"I, well, I," Lizzie stammered.

"Spit it out Lizzie, this is not the time for secrets. We need to be united as a family if we are to stop any suspicious talk," Mother said.

"Well," then in a mad rush she added, "I-think-I-can-do-that-too."

Mother smiled then. "It's alright Lizzie. You should have told me before, I can help you keep it hidden. You know almost everyone in the family has some sort of talent. We just have to be careful that no one suspects. They would think us all witches and as amusing as it sounds it wouldn't be funny at all if it happened."

"I used it on Alex earlier when he grabbed at the nettles, but I pretended it was the doc leaves that cured him. Is that the sort of thing you mean?" Lizzie asked.

"That is perfect. Always cover your actions with something else. Poultices are wonderful for that. Well done."

Molly gazed at her hand. The bandage had been removed a few hours after she wounded it and it was as if there never had been a cut. Gran? Gran could heal? She felt so stupid, how could she have not realised? The cut on her hand was healed and pain-free almost immediately. Certainly, she hadn't given it much thought since she came around after her faint.

Her attention was caught again when she heard Ghosts mentioned. She had missed some of what Mother said while she was thinking about Gran, but the mention of Ghosts had her listening intently.

"Yes, it was my Great Grandmother who saw the Ghosts and helped them," Mother was saying. "Occasionally it misses someone, but there is time yet for your skill to show itself Mary. My Mother had visions of the future, but her first vision didn't occur until after she was married. She saw Alex when I was no older than you Mary." Mother smiled to herself as she tussled the slight mop of hair on Alex's head.

"Visions of the future can be dangerous though. So I would not wish that on anyone. Some of our ancestors became insane and had to be locked away. Folks called them an Oracle, but the visions came too fast and they couldn't stop them. It's more a curse than a skill. Your Grandmother was fortunate, she only had visions occasionally."

"What does all this have to do with what Alex said though?" asked Lizzie.

"I am getting to that. I think this little man can see Ghosts. We just need to work out who the Ghost is and what it wants to let it rest. And if either of you feels something strange is happening, please, please don't keep it to yourself. We are family and can help each other."

Mary and Lizzie looked at each other. Silent messages passed between their eyes. They had to tell Mother about Molly and also that Mary could hear her.

Molly however was totally lost in thought. So much made sense now. How her Mum had howled and become hysterical when she found that Dad had gone out in the car on the day of his accident. How she disappeared that day too and didn't come back. Molly was sure her Mum had seen a vision of the accident. It had to be that. Was her Mum an Oracle? Did the visions come so fast she couldn't cope? That would explain why Gran only said it was grown-up stuff. No way would a child understand that. Even she at 15 was struggling with the concept. She would ask Gran if she ever got back home again. No, she couldn't think like that. Not if, but when she got home.

Turning her attention back to the family in front of her she continued to listen. She had missed the part where Mother had been told about Molly's existence, Mary was just telling about the bucket.

"So this Molly, is from the future? Not a Ghost at all." Mother looked at Alex with wonder.

"She sort of is a Ghost though Mother, we can't see her. Only Alex can," Mary said.

"Has she said why she's here Mary?" Mother asked.

Mary told Mother everything Molly had said about the tunnel and being stuck there. "I don't think she knows why she's here Mother."

"I'm listening, you know," Molly said indignantly. "You could talk to me instead of about me. I didn't just disappear, because your Mother appeared."

Molly hadn't meant to snap. Everything she was hearing was making sense to her. Helping her understand her own world better, but at the same time, she was frightened. She had visions too, but of the past. She could see and hear Ghosts and now she had travelled through time. Would she spend the rest of her life in some sort of asylum? She really felt the need for someone to put their arms around her and tell her it would be ok. That wasn't likely to happen until she got home. Being ignored felt like the last straw.

"Sorry, Molly." Mary did sound apologetic, but then she had to explain what Molly had said.

Even Mother looked sheepish. "Please join us at the table Molly," she pointed to a stool. "If you sit there we can look towards you when we speak. How wonderful that one of my great, great and so on grandchildren should visit with me. It is a pleasure to meet you."

Feeling guilty that she'd snapped at Mary, Molly remembered her manners. At first, she smiled then realising they couldn't see her do that, she said, "the pleasure is all mine." Mary became her echo.

"If you don't know why you're here, what do you think you need to do to get back?" Mother asked.

Molly was quiet for a moment, she wasn't sure what she should say. She couldn't tell them that Mary was going to be hanged as a witch. Maybe if she didn't mention names. Just tell it as Gran had told her. "I…have… to…stop a murder I think."

The colour drained from Mary's face as she looked at her family.

"What Mary? What did she say?" Mother asked.

Taking a deep breath Mary repeated what Molly said. Then the table was silent. Mother stood and walked the room. An index finger against her cheek, she said nothing just walked up and down.

Eventually, she stopped, "chamomile tea for everyone I think. Can Molly drink? She's not really a Ghost I guess, or is she? This is confusing."

"Oh, yes please, I would love a drink" Molly preferred hot chocolate, but she was sure that in this age such a thing wouldn't exist and although it wasn't her preferred drink, right now chamomile would be wonderful.

"Does she want some cake? I know it's not Sunday, but cake is for special occasions and I can't think of anything more special. I bet she's starving poor mite. We have a guest and should treat her as such. And…she is family," she added with a smile. "Lizzie put Alex down for the night. We have work to do and his seeing Molly is not helpful to us anymore." Then she set about making tea and cutting cake.

Once everything was on the table, Mother seemed to have reached a decision, but before she could tell it the cellar door opened. It was Lawrence.

"Sorry to interrupt your tea Mrs Barber, but I just wanted to be sure you were well. James told me what happened."

Mother rose from the table and moved to face Lawrence. "Thank you for your consideration sire, but we are quite well thank you."

Molly could see that she was torn between the courtesy of inviting him to stay and just wanting him out of there. Molly wanted him to leave as soon as possible, she didn't trust him as far as she could throw him and she knew that wasn't very far. All eyes in the room remained on him. Would he just go?

"If we can be of assistance, please don't hesitate to ask. What were the men after?" he said.

Mother had no choice, he obviously wasn't going to leave. "Would you care to join us? We were just having tea and cake to thank the good Lord that Mary stayed safe."

"Ah, no thank you. Your offer is most gracious, but dinner is waiting for me," he said. "So they were after Mary? Did they say why?"

Molly wanted to push him back through the door. He knew why, if James had told him what had happened. What was he doing here? After disdainfully glancing around the small room, his eyes had landed and stayed on Mary and he wasn't looking too kindly at her.

"Just a misunderstanding sire, nothing for you to worry over. If you don't mind…our tea is getting cold."

"Ah yes, sorry for the intrusion. I will walk back over the fields, a lovely evening for a walk don't you think?" and with a polite nod to Mother, he left by the outside door.

The candle on the table flickered as a collective sigh of relief sounded in the room. Mother returned to the cake and continued to portion it out, but Molly watched Lawrence through a gap in the curtains. He didn't leave as he said he was doing, but headed for the barn.

"Mary, Lawrence has headed into the barn. I think he's up to mischief. Let me out and I will watch him," Molly said.

Mary rose from the table and opened the door, just in time to see Lawrence exit the barn.

"Sorry Miss Mary, seems I got turned around. Don't know what I was thinking," he said as he headed away down the path.

"He was up to mischief Mary, I'm sure of it. Don't trust him," Molly said.

"Just going to check the barn Mother," Mary said.

Mother looked surprised, "Why?"

"Lawrence was in there," she replied.

"No Mary. Lizzie, you go. Mary, you don't leave this house alone until this is sorted." Mother looked determined, her chin set and eyes fiery. "This is just a little too scary for my liking. Lawrence has always been a weasel, even as a child. Something's not right here."

Lizzie left the house with a hooded candle and headed to

the barn. Everyone else watched through the window. Within a few minutes, Lizzie was back milking bucket and a plank of wood in hand. "There's vinegar in this bucket. That was definitely not there earlier. It will need a good clean before we milk Daisy again." She placed the bucket in the porcelain sink and taking the plank of wood said, "I think we should block the door for tonight, just in case."

Mother nodded and left Lizzie to the task as she looked at Mary with despair, "I can't very well accuse Lawrence without landing us all in trouble, but Mary if he is out to get you, you are going to have to be very careful what you do. Not only Mr Smith accusing you, but Lawrence seemingly siding with him. Promise me you will be cautious Mary."

"Of course Mother. And we have Molly to watch out too. She will tell us if anything strange is happening," Mary replied. "She was the one that told me about Lawrence being in the barn."

Although Mary sounded confident, Molly knew she must be quaking in her shoes. No matter how gently she had told of the murder, she knew Mary understood, she was the one that was murdered.

Mother smiled, "Thank you Molly, you saved us a lot of trouble there."

"Glad to be of service," Molly said, then cheekily to lighten the mood, "I think we were about to have tea and cake when we were so rudely interrupted. If it's alright I would really love some."

Mary relayed the message and then everyone started to

laugh. As the laughter died, Mother finished slicing the cake and Lizzie finished pouring the tea. They sat around the table in front of the blocked door, and once the family got over the strangeness of a teacup and cake lifting themselves, they took five minutes quiet to gather their thoughts.

Molly didn't know what the others were thinking, but she knew she was thinking this was the most delicious cake she had ever eaten. "Mary, will you put the recipe for this cake in your notebook? It's quite wonderful and I would like to learn to make it myself."

"How did you know about that?

"I found it, sorry but I read some of it already. I didn't know I was going to actually meet you."

Mother and Lizzie were looking at Mary waiting for explanations, but Mary decided there were some things they didn't need to know.

She nodded to where she could see cake disappearing piece by piece before saying, "Molly thinks your cake is delicious Mother."

Mother had been looking anxiously at Mary, scared for her youngest daughter's life, but the compliment brought a smile to her face.

"Right," Mother said after everyone had finished filling their faces and speech was possible again. "We need to sort this out before it becomes a disaster. We know Mr Smith is the ringleader. Grief is what is driving him, he needs someone to blame for his wife and baby's death. It is much easier to blame Mary than himself. As for Lawrence, I am not so sure what his beef with Mary is, but there is something."

At the blank looks from Mary and Lizzie, Molly interrupted. "Mr Smith was the one who got the rye. He didn't notice the Ergot and his wife and baby died because of it."

Molly waited while Mary repeated what she had said, so everyone knew. Mother started nodding. "Exactly. The thing is, what are we going to do about it?"

"I don't think there is much we can do tonight Mother," Lizzie said.

Molly felt frustrated, "can't you just go to the police? Won't they do something?"

Mary looked puzzled as she repeated what Mary had said. Lizzie and Mother frowned. "What are 'police', Molly?" Mary asked.

Molly was struck dumb, for once she had no reply. They didn't have police in the 1600s? She knew she had to say something, but she had just broken her first rule. Not to say anything they shouldn't know about.

Eventually, she said, "They stop people from stealing and things like that."

Mary smiled then, "Oh you mean the parish constable."

Mother's face brightened, "That's a good idea, he's a reasonable man. We could try him tomorrow. Lizzie, you could go and see if he is around. His farm is busy at this time of year though, so I'm not sure if he will have time for this."

It was agreed that Lizzie would go and Molly would stay by Mary's side at all times. The door would remain barricaded and no one would be allowed into the cottage.

Chapter 11

Molly sat the first part of the night keeping guard, but nothing happened. She checked out the cellar and all the different things the family stored there. Bottled fruits, dried meats, herbs galore, boxes of vegetables and potatoes, some gone to seed. "Gran would have loved to see this. We should use the cellar for storage just the same. It's so cold down here, like a huge fridge. And I should stop talking to myself."

Thoughts of Gran brought on a melancholy feel. Would she ever get back and see her again? She couldn't imagine being stuck as a Ghost forever. Aisha must be wondering what had happened to her by now and Gran must be beside herself with worry. The only thing she could do was protect Mary and hope she could save her and that would send her home again.

Thoughts of going home led Molly once more through the candlelit tunnel. "I wonder who keeps these candles burning?"

Once inside the Hall, she set off to explore again. She didn't bother trying to be quiet or hidden. She had to find Lawrence, find out what he was doing.

Passing maidservants and shoe boys she made her way through corridors and connecting rooms, but there was no sign of Lawrence. She wondered if he had gone to bed too. Upstairs she checked the bedrooms, knocking on closed doors to see if there was an answer before she opened them. The open ones she went in without knocking.

One room she knocked on was answered by a maid and she could see an older lady surrounded by more ladies, all sewing something. Needles flipping in and out of material making neat stitches. Molly guessed it to be James's mother and her ladies. She was older than Molly had expected, but then she considered how old Lawrence was and realised his Mother would have to be older than Mary's.

In another room she found James sleeping on a huge bed. He turned over in his sleep and Molly could understand why Mary was falling for him. He was very handsome and had a kind face. So different to his brother. Finally, she found Lawrence, in an annexe of a bedroom. He was talking with Mr Smith.

Holding a cap in his hands, Mr Smith kept bowing to Lawrence as he spoke. "I got the lads like we said, sire. It was your own brother m'lord who stopped us. And what with 'er mam being there too. Was impossible sire.

Lawrence looked thoughtful for a few minutes. Then glanced over his shoulder as if he suspected Molly's presence.

Molly held her breath. She knew he couldn't see or hear her, but still, she kept perfectly motionless. She strained to hear what was said, not daring to move, just in case he had a power too. She couldn't comprehend how the whole family could have them and no one else. Surely others would have them as well.

She caught just a few words from Lawrence as he laid out his plan to Mr Smith, "sack," "trap," and then with a sneer on his face and laughter in his voice he almost shouted as he finally added, "then we hang her from the old oak tree where she and

James would meet. No travelling to York for witch trials. We know she's a witch. That's not needed."

Molly finally understood how James had been blamed for betraying Mary. It all began to make sense to her. Poor James had been an unwitting pawn in his brother's hands. He must have been totally devastated by what happened.

Mr Smith left through a back stair. Molly didn't follow. Her anger was with Lawrence. How could he do that to someone his brother loved? Her anger boiled over, but as she couldn't do anything to Lawrence personally she took vengeance on his room.

She pulled all the bedding off his bed onto the floor and threw a pillow in his direction. Next, she emptied drawers and flung items around the room. Finally, she opened and closed a wardrobe door, slamming it hard each time she closed it. Feeling well satisfied she enjoyed the look of terror on his face as things moved in his room seemingly on their own. See if he can blame that on Molly she thought.

She left Lawrence's room with a slam of his door and headed downstairs to the kitchen. The cake had been delicious, and although she wasn't really hungry she did fancy something to nibble on. The kitchen was deserted. The fire was banked for the night, just embers slowly burning. Heading into the pantry Molly hunted for food. A pie looked delicious. She found a knife in a drawer and cut herself a slice. Sitting at the table munching on steak pie she looked at the knife and decided to keep it, she might need that if Mary was tied up. She found some cloth to wrap it in and then slipped it inside her sock.

As she sat drinking a glass of milk she spotted a mouse running towards the pantry. "You hungry too little one?" she asked it. The mouse stopped and seemed to assess her before running up a table leg and sitting to clean its paws in front of her.

"Either you can see me and are very brave, or you have no idea I am here. Which is it? Ok, I'll get you some cheese, wait there."

The mouse watched as Molly pilfered cheese and lay it on the table. "Take it to the other side please," Molly said.

Picking up a portion of the cheese the mice did as it was bid.

"You can understand me? Can you put some cheese on the chair?"

Taking another piece of cheese the mouse put it on the chair and then ran back to Molly. "This is amazing. I thought I understood the horse when I first got here. It must be my Ghost form. Or maybe it's my skill. How cool would that be."

Black eyes peered at her then it started to squeak.

"Oh, you have a family to feed? Ok show me where you need the cheese and I'll carry it for you."

Running back down the leg of the table the mouse ran to a small opening in the floorboards, gave a squeak and disappeared. Molly took a good portion of cheese from the pantry and placed it by the hole.

A small head poked out took a nibble of cheese and disappeared, followed by another head, then another, until all the cheese was gone.

"Well mister mouse, your family's fed, but I'm not sure how to help my family." She returned to her seat at the table to consider. It was obvious to her that the time of Mary's death was close. Too much was happening and Lawrence had made his plan already.

If she was to save Mary she had to make a plan of her own and to do that she needed to see the lay of the land in the 1600s. She knew the woods were different, but she needed to see the rest of the village. See what else had changed over time. Leaving the kitchen she headed outside. The moon shone, a full moon with a clear sky. Without light pollution thousands of stars reflected in her eyes. Visibility was amazing.

The gardens of the Hall looked similar in layout to what she was used to, but there were no signs of building works or houses in the distance. Fields and more fields. Woods and more woods. Smoke from chimneys indicated where a cottage or house might be found or maybe where someone was sleeping rough in the woods. The quietness was profound. The hoot of an owl, the discontented baa of a sheep and the howl of a distant dog were the only sounds. Molly was sure if she listened hard she would be able to hear insects and spiders, but not being too enamoured by either she didn't listen. She knew what she needed to do and under the light of the moon she set off to do it.

Chapter 12

Molly took great pleasure in watching a beautiful sunrise the next morning. The sky dyed an array of reds, pinks and purples. "Looking at that sky it'll probably rain later. Red sky at night, shepherds delight. Red sky at morn, shepherds warn. Yep, definitely a rain warning that one. But still, worth staying awake all night to see."

As she approached the cottage through the morning mist she saw Daisy cow. The cow must have brought herself back because everyone had been far too busy to even consider the animals.

Daisy mooed and Molly knew it was a greeting. A glad to see you. She had never milked a cow, she wouldn't know how to start, so after apologising to Daisy she headed over to the hen house. The least she could do was gather a few eggs for the family for breakfast.

Glancing about she saw how much thicker the woods were than in her own time. All the trees she could see now were gone in her time. Chopped away, making room for new houses, shops, roads and all the other man-made things she was used to. It felt strange not to see the village green and she knew old Mr Lewis' place didn't exist. It was like a whole new world.

Glancing at the cottage she noticed the curtains were open and smoke puthered from the chimney. The family were awake, it was time she got those eggs. The hens greeted her with clucks and as Molly asked them to move this way or that, they did it. She felt quite pleased with herself as she went back to the cottage with hands full of eggs.

As she got closer the smell of fresh bread clung in the air like nectar. Someone had bread cooking. She knocked on the door and shouted out, "it's me, Molly."

Mary called back and the door was opened and quickly closed and locked behind her.

"I bring eggs."

Lizzie gasped as five eggs appeared on the table in front of her, then gathering her wits, she grinned and said, "thank you."

With the arrival of eggs, the household busied themselves making breakfast. Dippy eggs and soldiers for Alex. A wooden high chair pulled to the table kept him contained. Fried egg sandwiches for everyone else. Molly wolfed it down, it seemed ages since the pie in the Hall. She seemed to be constantly hungry, but she wondered if she would ever get tired. She hadn't slept for over 24 hours and she was still wide awake. Time to sleep when this is finished she thought to herself.

After breakfast was done and cleared away Lizzie donned a light coat and prepared to visit the parish constable.

"Take Chestnut, it'll be faster," Mother said. "And remember to explain how Mrs Smith and the baby died. He must understand that Mary had nothing to do with it."

"I'll do my best, but I have to find him first. He could be anywhere," Lizzie replied. Then after giving Mary a hug she was gone.

The morning passed quietly, with no visitors of any kind.

Molly was on edge the whole time. Would Lizzie get help? When would the mob come? Would her plan work? Should she just tell the family the truth of what happened and see if they can stop it?

No, she couldn't tell them, Mary would live in fear. The whole family would place themselves in lockdown. Living with doors locked and never going outside or leaving Mary alone for a second was no way to live. No, she couldn't tell them what was coming. She just had to be there when it happened and stop it.

She recalled what Ghost Mary said. Mother had gone to the Hall, Lizzie was out gathering herbs and she was making dinner. Those three things together were the key, she had to look out for that, but there was also James who unknowingly entrapped her. Ghost Mary had never said what he did. Had he been the one come calling while she made dinner and persuaded her to go outside?

Mary stayed indoors the whole morning. She was never left alone. As the day progressed and nothing happened, the door was unlocked and opened to let in the fresh air. Mary gave frequent nervous glances outside, but said nothing.

"Don't worry Mary I'm here, I'll be with you always," Molly tried to reassure her, but she only received a tight smile in return. She'd obviously realised that Molly was there to prevent her murder and that scared her.

Lizzie returned just before lunch. Banging on the door, she yelled "Let me in, quick."

Mother ran to the door and unlocked it letting a dishevelled

Lizzie fall past her. "What? Lizzie, what happened?"

"Quick hide. The bolt hole. Soldiers chasing me," she gasped.

Mother wasted no time. "Mary, help me. Lizzie, go and get Alex," she said as she moved towards the dresser. She and Mary bent down and each lifted one side of the scatter rug. It was fastened to a trap door that led under the floor. Lizzie had run upstairs and grabbed Alex from his crib where he was napping and together they descended into the bolt hole. As they pulled the trap door closed behind them the carpet fell into place.

Molly watched in amazement. The house looked empty. The door had been left unlocked, so it looked for all the world as if the people who lived here had run away. She moved to go outside and see what was happening, but before she could the sounds of many feet trampling across the mud outside and shouting voices reached her.

"She can't have gone far."

"Been a while since we had us a woman, tasty she is too."

"Aye, come out li'l darlin', we got some nice games you can play with us.

One of the soldiers pushed the door open. "Hey lads, come on, maybe she's hiding in here.

"Well, that's her horse so she can't be far away. Maybe she's lying on a bed waiting for us." The sound of hoots and laughter followed.

Molly cringed, her stomach recoiled as she watched three men in soldiers' uniforms, covered in dirt and grime, stinking like a cesspit, stomp through the cottage. There must be something she could do, somehow she needed to get them to leave.

Slamming the door shut caused them to jump, but then they started to laugh, "Must be the wind. A sure sign we're on the right track."

One of them went into the pantry, "Hey guys look ye here, a fancy cake. Looks started on, but plenty left. Who wants a piece?"

One soldier was coming downstairs, "No one up here, so we may as well make ourselves at home. She's bound to come back and cake while we wait, why not?"

Molly was appalled, these men were scumbags. Standing by the man in the pantry, she moved the cake across the shelf just as he reached for it.

"What!" he said, stepping back.

"Wassup man?"

"The cake, it... moved."

"Don't be so daft, Rob. Bring it out here. Partial to a bit of cake I am."

"I'm tellin' ya it did. You come and get it."

Rob moved out of the pantry and let the other man in.

Just as the other man reached for it, Molly moved it again. It seemed such a simple trick to her, but the look on the men's faces was priceless. She started to laugh to herself as she moved the cake quickly backwards and forwards.

"Just leave it Cooper, let's get out of here. Maybe that girl's a witch. She did just up and vanish and now this. Sarg wanted us at t'other side of the hill by sunset anyhow." Rob was looking very pale as he edged his way towards the outside door.

Just then the other man appeared. He had been searching drawers and cupboards, looking for Molly didn't know what, but guessed it would be anything valuable. "What you two up to in there?"

"We were trying to get some cake, but blow me down if this cake ain't enchanted. We can't grab it for love nor money," Cooper replied.

"That's 'cos you two haven't got the brains you were born with, shift over."

Once again Molly started to move the cake, but this guy was fast and soon had it in his hands. "Nothing to it. See it's not enchanted at all. You two are thick as treacle. Come on, let's enjoy this and if she's not back when we're done then we'll just have to call here on our way back or Sarg'll have our guts for garters."

The man placed the cake on the table, but Molly wasn't done. Three mouths dropped open as the cake floated across to the pantry and placed itself back on the shelf.

"I'm not staying here," Cooper said and all three soldiers ran to the door and outside. From the doorway, Molly laughed and shouted after them, "Good riddance to bad rubbish," as she watched them run down the mud path and far away from the little cottage.

She closed the door and shouted to Mary, "You should be safe now, they've gone."

The trapdoor opened a crack and eyes peered through the gap before it was flung back and with Mother leading, the family clambered out of the bolt hole. They looked nervously about them as they moved into the room, but it was as calm and tidy as when they had left it. "What happened?" Mother asked.

Molly proceeded to tell them what she had done, which Mary repeated between fits of laughter. Soon the whole room was in an uproar. Lizzie wiped tears from her eyes as she tried to keep a straight face to thank Molly, but it wasn't happening and she was soon laughing again.

"I don't think they'll be back any time soon, thank goodness," said Mother as she sank into the hearthside chair. "The bolt hole worked perfectly though. It's a good job your dad thought to do that."

The chatter became all about the bolt hole and how safe they had felt hidden right beneath the feet of the soldiers. Then Lizzie told how she had come across the soldiers on her way back from looking for the village constable. They had pulled at her clothes trying to drag her from the horse, but she had managed to stay mounted and raced for home. Not being a good rider though she couldn't go too fast, so they had been able to keep up.

"What happened with the constable?" Mary asked.

Lizzie looked at the floor before glancing up at Mary. "I'm sorry Mary, I hunted everywhere I could think of, but I couldn't find him. Then I met George, you know the blacksmith. He said the constable was heading to see someone in Sheffield. I must have just missed him. He won't be back for a few days."

"Let's hope he takes care, much of the war is being fought around there, and the last thing he needs is soldiers like the ones

Lizzie came across," Mother said.

"It's alright Lizzie, don't worry," Mary said as her bottom lip trembled and she bit down on it, her eyes watered, but she didn't cry. Mother put an arm around her, "now don't fret, we can manage, we have Molly our secret weapon.

Molly tried to sound cheerful and reassuring as she added her support to those of the rest of the family, but she felt far from cheerful. This was all going to be down to her. She had to keep her wits about her and be on constant alert.

As Molly had predicted, the afternoon was filled with rain. A heavy downfall, the wind picked up and blew the rain in sheets against the cottage. The door was locked again and the family spent some pleasant hours playing draughts and backgammon. Molly joined in, which they found really funny when the pieces started to move by themselves.

By nightfall, everyone except Molly was totally relaxed. It seemed the crisis was over. Mother encouraged everyone to have an early night. Lizzie brought Daisy back to the shed and bedded her down while Mary gathered the hens to the hen house and was just latching the door when it happened.

A sound behind her alerted Mary that she wasn't alone. She turned, but it was too late. A hand covered her mouth and then all was darkness.

Molly had been with Mary, but even she hadn't heard anything. She had been gazing around, looking at the differences that time had made to the cottage she knew as home. She spun around just in time to see Mr Smith and some of the other villagers throw a sack over Mary and carry her off.

Mary tried to scream, but the sacking muffled her cries. The only witness to what had happened was Molly and she couldn't tell anyone. Molly ran to the cottage, threw the door open so they would see Mary was gone and then she gave chase. She had to help, although she had no clue how.

The villagers stopped deep in the woods. The man carrying Mary over his shoulder threw her to the ground and the sack was removed.

"Put a gag on her you fool," Mr Smith said. "Witches can say things, you want warts for the rest of your life?"

Molly could hear Lizzie and her Mother shouting for Mary, but there was no way she could tell them where she was.

A toothless man looking like his head was upside down, hair on his chin and none on top, produced a handkerchief and tied it securely around Mary's mouth. Rope tied her hands behind her and feet together. "No running off for you and no shouting or cursing," he said.

Molly looked around. There were five men, none of them smelling too good and one looked ill, she hoped he wasn't contagious. The last thing she wanted was to catch some dreadful disease off one of these men.

"I'm here Mary," she said. Even giving Mary that bit of comfort seemed very little. What could she do?

Mr Smith was speaking, "I heard in the courts for witches in York, they test them. We need to see if the good Lord accepts her. If she belongs to the Devil, no harm can come to her."

One of the men spoke up, "how's that work then? If no

harm can come to her, what we supposed to do? And if the Lord accepts her, ain't it a bit late? Likely she be dead by then.

"Now stop your yabbering Joe, it's easy. If she belongs to the Devil then hanging or burning is the way to do it. It's the only way."

Mary started to struggle as she heard the word dead. She fought the ropes, but the more she struggled the tighter they became. Tears trickled down her cheeks, her face pale with fear.

"Wait Mary, I'll unfasten them, but don't move until I tell you to. Don't let them see you're free." Molly said.

Moving behind Mary she tried to unfasten the knots, but the pulling and tugging Mary had done made them too tight. "I can't get them undone, let me try your feet, at least then you can run."

Molly unfastened the ropes tying Mary's feet together leaving the ropes free but not obviously undone. Next, she loosened the gag on her mouth, leaving the handkerchief loose around the back of her neck. Mary could easily spit it away. She would need a knife to cut her hands loose, there was no way she was going to get those knots undone. Then she remembered the knife she had taken from the Hall. Reaching down to her sock she pulled out the knife. With the use of the knife, the rope fell away and Mary was free.

"I will distract them, they don't see me so I can scare them. Once they are really scared, run, your life truly depends on it."

Molly moved away from Mary and back to where the men were huddled and still debating the best way to see if Mary was a witch.

"They use ducking stools, I heard that," said another man. "If they drown they ain't no witch."

"Bah, you be daft you be," said the one with the upside-down head. "She'll be dead then and her Ma ain't liking to help us anymore if we kill her bairn and she is no witch. Ya all be knowing Missis Barber she looks out for us. What we gonna do if she doesn't help with the birthin' and stuff. We gotta do this right."

"I tell you, she's a witch, we should just hang her and be done with it," said Mr Smith as he lifted a drinking flask to his lips.

Molly took her chance. Grabbing the flask from his hands she moved it just out of his reach. Then trailed it through the air around the men. They couldn't see her, just the flask moving on its own. Throwing it to the floor she picked up a broken branch and started to hit the men with it. "Now Mary, run," she yelled.

The men screamed and ran, each in their own direction. Molly chose Mr Smith and gave chase, catching his bottom with the stick. She didn't hurt him, but from his squeals, she knew he thought he was running for his life.

Glancing back she could see that Mary had taken her chance and was running back to the cottage. Once Mary had disappeared from view, Molly gave Mr Smith another slap with the stick, before stopping her chase and heading towards the cottage herself. It was dark and this part of the woods didn't exist in Molly's time. She listened for the sounds of Lizzie and her Mother calling Mary to guide her the right way back to the cottage. She heard when Mary reached them, "phew," she said aloud. "That was close."

Molly found herself in pitch blackness. The calling from Lizzie and her Mother had stopped. She had no idea if she was heading in the right direction or totally the wrong way. Pulling her torch from her jeans pocket she switched it on. The trees around her threw shadows everywhere with torchlight. She circled around looking for the right way to go. Then the torch started to flicker. Molly banged it on her hand just as it went out.

"Dam! The batteries must have gone."

Slipping the torch back into her jeans, she let her eyes adjust to the blackness again. She had to think, there must be a way to find the cottage without lights. There hadn't always been street lighting to help people through the dark.

Leaning against the bark of a tree she stopped to consider her options. She could just sit and wait until daylight, but that would mean leaving Mary without her protection. Not really an option. A squirrel disturbed by the noise below was barking and kuking at her. "Oh shush," she told it. "I won't hurt you. Go back to sleep." The squirrel scurried closer, moving its head from side to side as if wondering who this was.

"Yes, I know you can see me. The mouse made that pretty clear. I won't bother you, I just need to think, now shush."

It scurried down to her and with a sigh, she put out her arm so it could jump on. Molly didn't move but just stared in wonder. She hadn't really expected it to do that. To be so close to a squirrel was amazing. After dropping a hazelnut in her hand it scurried back to the tree. Molly glanced up. A whole family of squirrels were watching. She couldn't believe her eyes as they scurried one after another to the ground, then climbing up her they dropped a nut in turn, before running back up the tree.

She looked up the tree trying to spot them again. She couldn't see them, but she did see stars. Lots of stars.

"Of course, if I find the north star I can head west to the cottage. I know we were running east."

Storing the hazelnuts in her jeans pocket, she thanked the squirrels before moving. Setting off carefully through the woods, looking through the tree branches eventually she found the north star.

"There! Now I need to go west, so turn left."

Moving slowly so as not to run into any trees in the pitch blackness, Molly eventually came to a clearing. The cowshed was in front of her. Now she just needed to follow the path Mary had used earlier that day and she should be back at the cottage.

She tried the cottage door, but it was locked. She knocked on the door, but there was no answer. She heard scuffles inside. Molly realised they must think it was the men coming back for Mary. "Mary," she called out, "it's me, Molly. Let me in."

She heard whispers and saw a curtain twitch as someone checked who was outside. Molly knew they wouldn't see anyone. Then the sound of furniture moving from behind the door. They must have barricaded it.

"Molly?" Mary said. Her voice held a quiver, she was still very frightened.

"Yes it's me, please let me in."

The door swung open and Molly dashed inside. "Close it I'm in."

The door was slammed shut and locked and the table was pushed back against it.

"I don't know where you are Molly, but thank you. From the bottom of my heart thank you," Mary said. Her eyes were red-rimmed and puffy, but the colour was back in her cheeks and judging by the dampness on Mother's shoulder she had had a lot of hugs to help her calm down.

The family sat together, drinking tea and reassuring each other that everything was going to be fine well into the night. Mary still looked pale but she could manage a smile. "We should try to sleep a while," said Mother. "The doors are barred, there is no way for anyone to get in without a great deal of noise. Come on you can both sleep in with me tonight."

The fire was banked. After wishing Molly a good night, they disappeared upstairs, leaving her by the side of the fire wondering what to do with her time. She still wasn't tired.

She couldn't play board games on her own. Looking around the cottage she wondered what she would do if she were at home. Then she knew how she could help. Poultices and potions. She would spend the rest of the night making them. She hunted around for paper and something to write with.

A drawer contained a course form of paper, but there was nothing to write with. Glancing around, her gaze took her back to the fire. If she could pull out some of the partially burnt wood, that would work. It was a form of charcoal. She would have to be careful not to burn herself and it would likely smudge a lot, so she would need to take great care with her writing.

Using a poker, she pulled out a small piece of wood and left it to cool on the hearth. She hunted and found a book containing recipes and then just before she set to work she wrote a note for Lawrence and slipped it into her jeans pocket.

The work was simple enough and gave Molly time to think. Twice now she'd heard mention of war and then there were the soldiers. What war could they be talking about? War of the Roses was before this time she was sure. She wished she had taken more notice of history at school. Could it be the Civil War? She couldn't remember when that had happened. She hadn't heard any fighting and when she was exploring last night she hadn't seen any sign of war. Of course, things would move slower in the 1600s than in her time. Just something else to be cautious of.

By the time the family woke at dawn all the herbs in the pantry had been turned to either a poultice or a potion and labelled and Molly was sat lazily by the fire feeling very pleased with herself.

To say Mother was happy would probably be an understatement. She enthused about her wonderful great, great and so many more greats granddaughter for a full hour after breakfast, until Lizzie begged for her to shut up.

The family seemed in really good spirits as though the horrors of the last couple of days had never happened. Mary was singing, Lizzie was spinning Alex around causing bubbles of laughter from his toothy mouth and Mother never stopped smiling as she watched her children.

All the chores were done when there was a knock on the pantry door.

The room went silent, even Alex had a look of concern.

Mother answered, "who is it?"

"James."

A huge sigh of relief went through the room, as Mary unlocked the door and after ushering James through, locked it again.

"What's going on?" he asked. "That door's never locked."

After offering James some tea, Mother explained what had happened to Mary, leaving out the part about Molly. She was more difficult to explain. Even James would have considered Mary a witch if he knew she could talk with spirits.

"Are you alright Mary-mol?" he said with a frown.

She smiled and nodded. His shoulders relaxed as he believed her.

"I came to see if you wanted to go for a walk, I brought a basket for a picnic lunch, but maybe we should stay in, or sit in the barn? What do you think?"

Chapter 13

Mary glanced at her Mother. She didn't know what to do. She really wanted to go on a walk with James, but would she be safe?

"Just go to the barn Mary," Molly said. "If you sit up in the rafters no one will know you are there and it's something you never do, so no one will think to look for you there."

Mary put the suggestion to James as though she had thought of it and everyone agreed it was a brilliant idea.

Mother exited the cottage first and scouted around to make sure there was no one around. Deciding it was safe she signalled to Mary and James. Molly followed, looking and listening for anyone lurking around all the time as they crossed over to the barn. All was quiet.

Mary and James climbed the ladder to the rafters where straw covered the wooden floor. James laid out a blanket and then produced cheeses, meats and pickled vegetables which he placed on the blanket. Buns and biscuits followed with apples and pears to finish. It looked like a feast even to Molly's eyes.

Sitting side by side on the straw they started to eat. Mary looked delirious in her happiness. Casting shy glances at James eventually she spoke. "This is wonderful James. Is it a special day or something? I have never seen so much food."

Turning to Mary he lowered his eyes, " I err... I have something...I was going to ask."

Mary started to laugh. "This isn't like you to be stuck for words. Whatever it is just spit it out. You know if I can help you I will."

"No, it's not that," James said. Taking a big breath he rose and went down on one knee. Mary gasped.

"You know there will never be another woman for me, Mary. I could never feel the same for another that I feel for you. I love you and would ask you to be my wife."

As Mary stuttered, he added, "I know it will be difficult, but if my family doesn't like it then I will leave them all. You are the most important thing to me. Please say yes." James lowered his eyes again, then looked up to see the tears that ran down Mary's face along with a huge smile.

"Is that a yes?" he asked, hope lit up his eyes.

Molly held her breath. She had never seen anything so beautiful in her life. The love that the two of them had was heart-wrenching. Even Molly had a tear in her eye. She knew she should go and leave the two lovers alone, but it was compulsive viewing. What would Mary say?

"You know I love you James. I think I have since the first moment I met you. Would your family even consider allowing you to marry me though? If they don't, they will cut you off. You will be penniless. What would you do?"

"Oh Mary, I don't care about them or their money. Grandmother left me a trust fund which I receive on the day I marry. It would tide us over until I can find work. I can read and write and so can you. That sort of work pays well. We would be fine, please say yes."

Throwing her arms around James's neck Mary squealed. "Yes, oh yes, yes I will."

Then they were kissing, a long lingering kiss.

Molly turned away. She didn't need to see that. She was heading to the ladder to climb down from the rafters when James started to speak again.

"I got you this. I didn't think a ring was appropriate yet. I didn't want my family to know until we were ready to tell them."

Turning around Molly saw James holding the pocket watch out to Mary. "A token of my love for you and the promise I made to you today. We will be married."

Mary's mouth was agape, she stuttered before saying, "It's beautiful, thank you." Then they were kissing again and Molly knew she should leave, but she couldn't resist being the first to say, "Congratulations," before heading to the barn door to keep a lookout.

Molly sauntered around the grounds of the cottage, listening all the time for signs of trouble. She waved to the squirrels and mice as she went. A hawk flew overhead and the small creatures hid as it sent a greeting to Molly. This was a bonus of being a Ghost that Molly hadn't expected. A badger poked its head out of a sett as Molly passed, acknowledging her with a nod.

Molly was so entranced by the animals, she almost forgot to keep listening for trouble. Looking around, she couldn't see any sign of other humans.

Leaves had started to turn on the trees. Reds, oranges and

gold lit the woods in a blaze of fire where the sun hit them. It was beautiful. Molly took time to just enjoy the peace and tranquillity that she hadn't had since heading into the tunnel.

She didn't stray too far from the barn, keeping it in sight all the while and was instantly aware when James and Mary came through the barn doors, holding hands. Smiling to herself she rushed over, "All clear Mary, you are safe to go back to the cottage."

Mary nodded her understanding, but James searched left and right, making sure there was no one around before letting go of Mary's hand. Placing his hand into the small of her back he ushered her towards the cottage and safety.

Molly grinned from ear to ear as she listened to them telling Mother and Lizzie about the engagement. They both promised to keep it a secret as they oohed and aahed over the pocket watch.

In the bottom of the picnic basket, James had hidden a bottle of elderberry wine and cups were brought out so they all could toast the engagement.

After James had gone, there was much chatter about future weddings for both Lizzie and Mary. All thoughts of the threat to Mary were forgotten. For the first time, Molly could be included in the conversation and she went into reams of descriptions to tell of the wonderful proposal. Mary blushed as she recited what Molly had to say about it.

"Haha, you forgot I was there didn't you?" Molly said.

"To be truthful, yes I did." Then Mary had to explain to Mother and Lizzie what they were talking about.

Alex waking from his nap stopped all the merriment and laughter and had Mother in business mode again. Lizzie was set to sweep the cottage and Mary was put to looking after Alex while she went to milk Daisy and check for more eggs.

Molly stayed with Mary and played with Alex, more high-fives and funny faces had him chuckling until Mary had prepared his milk and some carrot to munch on.

Mother was soon back with a bucket full of milk and a pocket full of eggs. She took them down into the cellar to store where it was cool and would keep them fresh.

A knock on the door sent them all once more into panic, but a peek through the window showed an elderly lady with a basket. Mother answered it while Mary dashed upstairs with Alex, out of the way.

Molly watched and called upstairs to Mary what was happening.

"Just an elderly lady wanting a potion for her arthritis. She's brought some potatoes in way of payment."

Mary returned to the living room with Alex and the day continued as a normal one should. Mary smiled more than usual, but other than that nothing else happened.

Molly hadn't forgotten the letter she'd penned for Lawrence. She needed to take it to the Hall and make sure he received it, but she was loath to leave Mary. Such an exciting day could turn into a disaster at any moment.

It was as if Mary could read her thoughts, "You don't need to stay here all the time you know Molly. Mother and Lizzie will watch over me. You should have a look around, I'm sure things are very different now from what they will be in the future. You should explore."

After assuring Mary that she would only be an hour or so and Mary promising to stay in the cottage Molly set off once more through the passageway to the Hall. She had already explored the area while the family had slept, but she did need to visit the Hall again.

Opening the door at the end of the passageway just a crack she could hear voices. One was Lawrence, but the other she didn't recognise. She listened.

"But Father, you don't understand. Someone has to stay here and keep an eye on James. You and Caleb are off fighting the war. Mother is... well you know how Mother is with him. He can do no wrong."

"Don't you disrespect your Mother boy. You are not too old for the stick. Your Mother is a fine woman, perfectly capable of watching over James and the staff are here too. No harm will come to him and what mischief can he get up to? No, you need to take up your duties. You are an idle fop who needs to accept some responsibility. That is the end of the subject. You will attend court tomorrow. You will attend His Majesty as requested."

Molly couldn't help the smile that lit her face. Lawrence was leaving, which would make life much more tolerable. Maybe now she didn't need to leave him that note. He wouldn't be able to harm Mary from afar.

It seemed Lawrence was far from finished with the conversation though. Just as Molly was pulling the door closed in preparation to leave, he started to speak again.

"I will go to court as instructed Father, but who will stop Mary from bewitching James? Someone needs to keep a handle on his whereabouts. They are getting far too close for my comfort."

"Who is this Mary? James has found someone?" Father said.

"Mrs Barber's daughter, sir. He is besotted, she must have bewitched him. I can think of no other reason for this nonsense," Lawrence replied.

"Hmm, I will have a word with him. It will stop now. You will still go to court."

Molly heard footsteps and a door slam. She had no idea who had left and if someone was still in the room. Did she dare enter? Chewing on her lip she considered while she listened for any sounds of someone still there. All was silent. Carefully she opened the door a bit more and popped her head out. She wasn't frightened they would see her, but they would see the door move and know someone was listening.

Lawrence stood with his back to her. Quickly opening the door, she slipped out and closed it again. He must have heard. Turning he strode over and checked the door, yanking it open as if to surprise someone. Shaking his head he closed it again and left the room following in his father's footsteps.

Molly knew that leaving a note for Lawrence to try to frighten him, would do no good now. His father was also trying to stop the union. The only thing she could do was warn James.

She had seen Lawrence writing in the drawing room. She

should be able to find a pen and paper there. All the doors were ajar so she had little problem moving around the Hall. Moving swiftly she entered the drawing room to find Lawrence talking with the butler.

"Take this note to Mr Smith and tell him he must do this today. I will be gone tomorrow, so it must be today," Lawrence said.

"Erm, if I may sir, do what?" the butler asked.

"None of your concern, he will know. Go swiftly." Lawrence turned away, the butler was dismissed.

The butler looked at the note in his hand and shook his head as he left the drawing room. "Old Smithy doesn't read, how's he supposed to know what it says?" he muttered to himself.

Molly felt some reassurance that if Mr Smith couldn't read things might not go as Lawrence planned, but she couldn't take that risk. She needed to move fast. Lawrence was on a deadline which meant he was even more dangerous than before.

Lawrence sat on one of the sofas with his back to the writing table. Molly found herself some paper, took the quill and dipped it in the inkpot. Splodges of ink dripped onto the paper. She tapped the quill on the inkpot and started to write, biting at her lip as she concentrated. She had only managed to write James when the ink ran out. She tried again, remembering to tap the quill on the inkpot. After numerous attempts and lots of splodges, she managed a note.

James,
    Mary is in danger from your Father and Lawrence.

They are accusing her of witchcraft. You must protect her.
A friend.

After blotting the ink she folded it and put it in her pocket. As she turned with the intention of finding James she saw Lawrence, looking at the writing table, his face alabaster white. He had obviously seen the pen moving on its own. Molly couldn't help the chuckle as she headed towards the stairs to find James.

She went towards the kitchens first. That is where she would have spent all her time if she lived here. The kitchen was a bustle of activity, but there was no sign of James. Looking through the window she could see some of the grounds, but they were huge and she hoped he wasn't out there. She headed upstairs, checking each room as she went. "Where could he be? He must be somewhere."

Her tour eventually took her to James' bedroom. The door was closed. She knocked, but there was no answer. She tried the door, it opened with ease and she went in. James wasn't there so she lay the note on his pillow and after a quick glance round in admiration of such a lovely room, she headed for the door. "Time to get back to Mary. I'm sure the time is very near. It has to be if Lawrence is leaving tomorrow."

At that moment a maid went past. "Master James' door has opened itself again. I'll lock it so the cat doesn't get in. That just wouldn't do with his allergy."

Another voice replied, "Good idea, that last episode almost did for him. If it wasn't for Mrs Barber... Leave the key, or he won't be able to get in again."

Molly dashed for the door but she was too late. The door slammed shut and a key turned. She stared at the door and then tried the handle, pulling and tugging, but she knew it was fruitless. The door was locked.

Running to the window she looked out. She tried the window and it slid open with ease, but as she leaned out she knew she couldn't get out that way. She was far too high up and there wasn't so much as a drainpipe to shimmy down.

Glancing around the room for inspiration she looked at the bed. Could she tie the sheets and use them as a rope? "Don't be stupid Molly. Like as not you would break your neck." What could she do? She couldn't protect or help Mary if she was stuck in James' bedroom.

Someone would come eventually, that she was sure of, but she had told Mary she wouldn't be long and she didn't think she had very long to prevent the hanging from happening. Anything could happen while she was stuck in here. She wrung her hands as she marched a path between the door and window. "Wearing a hole in the floor is not a solution Molly. Come on girl think. And stop talking to yourself."

James had a sofa under the window facing the door. She sat down and stared at the door willing it to open. It didn't. 20 minutes later and it still hadn't opened. Molly had paced, sat and paced some more. She needed to do something but she had no idea what.

She chewed her lip. Looking around the bedroom for inspiration the dawning of an idea came to her. If she could poke out the key could she catch it on the note she had left for

James and drag it under the door?

She checked the gap under the door. It wasn't overly large but it could be enough, she hoped. Now she needed something to push the key with. There was nothing obvious laid around, so she started to search his drawers.

"A broken conker? Nah. Why would he keep that? Must be love," Molly said with a laugh. "What else is in here? A ribbon? Pocket watch? Nope can't use any of those." She shuffled a Bible around and then she saw it, a pair of scissors. Small and pointy. Perfect.

Taking the note off the pillow she opened it out and laid it flat on the floor in front of the door. Making sure it was directly under the keyhole she slid it under the door to the other side. Kneeling on the floor she poked the scissors through the keyhole until they hit the key, and then she started to push. The key didn't move at first. She jostled the scissors around and tried again. After a few tries, the key started to move. Keeping her hand as steady as she could she pushed gently and firmly until the key fell from the hole.

Crossing her fingers and saying a small prayer first she took a hold of the paper and slowly pulled it towards her. She heard the key hit the door. It was too big it wouldn't come through. She wanted to cry, tears filled her eyes. So close and yet so far.

Dropping her head to her hands to dash away the useless tears she spotted a warp in the door. A place in the centre where the gap underneath was just a bit bigger. Would it be big enough?

With hope in her heart, she gently slid the paper and key

towards the warp. The post of the key slid under the door as she pulled the paper towards her, but the head of the key refused to go past it.

Taking hold of the key post she waggled it up and down until her fingers were sore. She could see the warp taking damage and the floor beneath the door was wearing down, but it was so slow. She moved the key to the other hand and continued.

"Yes!" Molly shouted. The key was in her hand. She was free.

After placing the note back on James' pillow and closing the window, she unlocked the door and set off running through the Hall to get back to the cottage. She had been gone for hours and it was now well into the afternoon. Anything could have happened.

She raced down the tunnel and climbed the cellar steps coming up in the pantry. Mother, Lizzie and Alex were there, but there was no sign of Mary. Where could she be? How could Molly find out? No one there could hear if she asked.

"Alex?" Molly looked at him. Would he tell them she was there?

She aimed a high five at Alex and he started to giggle. "Laaybee," he said through his giggle.

Mother turned her attention to Alex, "Is Molly here Alex?"

"Laaybee," he said again, reaching out for Molly.

"Mary's just gone for a walk with James, Molly. I don't think he can stay away from her now they are betrothed. He promised to look after her. I think they were heading for the oak tree. They shouldn't be very long, they've been gone 15 minutes already."

Molly couldn't think of anything worse to have happened. Not considering those inside the cottage, she flung open the door and ran out after them.

She caught up with them just as James and Molly headed into the gap in the oak tree. The tree wasn't nearly as huge as in Molly's time. The gap was much larger, it looked like it had been hit by lightning, scorched edges to a yawning hollow. Over the years the tree had grown and the gap had been closed, which was why Molly hadn't been able to just walk in.

Everything looked fine. There was no sign of anyone close by. She called to Mary that she was there and a small wave from behind Mary's back showed she had been heard.

Keeping her distance, Molly sat with her back against another tree. Pulling a long piece of grass she stuck an end in her mouth and chewed it, then thinking of Aisha and the last time she saw her, she removed it. She wasn't a cow.

She wondered about Aisha and Gran, what would they think? They must have missed her by now. Aisha would have been trying to phone her. Gran would be frantic, knowing Molly had gone in the tunnel, then just vanished. It was no good worrying about it though, there was nothing she could do. She hoped when she'd helped Mary she would somehow just go home. She wasn't a big technology fan, but she loved indoor plumbing and the luxury of hot water on tap. A fire in one room to stave off the cold was not the same as central heating all over the house. She even missed the luxury of pen and paper which she hadn't known was a luxury. She really missed the 21st century.

She didn't realise how long she'd been daydreaming until she saw James and Molly emerge from the tree, laughter on their lips and an empty basket in Mary's hands. It was time to go back to the cottage.

Keeping her distance, Molly followed.

They hadn't gone very far when Lawrence appeared between the trees ahead of them. Molly was instantly on alert. She looked around, but couldn't see anyone else, he seemed to be on his own.

Leaving Mary alone, James marched over to confront his brother. He hadn't forgotten the conversation they had about him not seeing Mary. Or the tattle tale he had done to Father. He fully intended to put his brother in his place.

Mary waited where she was for a moment, but when she saw Lawrence put an arm around James and lead him away from her, out of sight in the trees. She called out, "James?" There was no answer.

Molly was unsure what to do, James had promised to protect Mary, but he was walking away from her. "Mary, run for home. Now!" she yelled. She wouldn't take a chance with Mary's safety.

She was still unsure though, should she follow James and Lawrence, find out what was going on, or stick with Mary? The decision was made for her when Mary started to run after James, completely ignoring Molly's warning.

"No! Mary come back, run home." Molly shook her head

to herself as she gave chase.

Charging ahead of Mary, Molly managed to catch up with them first. James was being pulled along by Lawrence now. His hands were tied together and a ball of something was stuffed in his mouth, preventing him from giving any warning to Mary. Lawrence had a knife wedged between them out of sight. If he struggled Lawrence would wound him, possibly fatally. "So much for brotherly love," Molly muttered. She looked around, the woods had become eerily silent, with no bird song, no crickets, no sound but for a slight rustle of leaves in the wind. "Run Mary, run. It's a trap."

This time Mary listened and dropping the picnic basket picked up her skirt and set off running towards the cottage. Molly followed listening all the time. An alarm call from a squirrel told Molly the way was blocked. "Not that way Mary, run around."

Mary ran back towards the oak tree, her breathing coming hard and fast. Her heart pounded in her chest. Ducking inside the gash of the oak Mary hid. The horror of her situation had not been lost on her. Tears ran in rivulets down her cheeks, but there seemed nowhere for her to go.

Standing outside the oak Molly watched for danger. "Try to slow your breathing Mary. I can hear you, and if I can so can others."

Molly was confused, it didn't happen like this. They should have been fine. None of the signs had been there. What had gone wrong? She knew worrying about that now wouldn't help them. She had to get Mary out of there. She could hear the sounds of men thrashing their way through trees and hitting bushes with sticks. Taunting calls of, "come out little witch" and "witchy, witchy where are you," sounded loud to Molly's ears. She could only imagine the fear Mary felt.

The men were getting closer, Molly didn't know how she could divert them. Ghost Mary had diverted her away, by causing a shadow, but Molly didn't know how to do that. It wasn't an option. The animals were hiding so she couldn't use them. If she ran through the bushes though, the men would hear and think it was Mary. It was worth a try even though it meant leaving Mary alone for a few minutes.

After telling Mary what she was doing and reminding her to stay hidden, Molly set off. She rustled every bush, trampled ferns, squashed moss and left signs of her passing on grass and sedges. Anything that might make a noise she made sure it did. The men had to think it was Mary running.

Once she was sure men were headed her way she detoured quietly and carefully back towards the oak tree, arriving just in time to see Mary being hauled out by her hair, her screams shattered the air.

Men surrounded her, taunting her with malicious words of how she would die a witch's death as they dragged her across the coarse ground.

"Got you now little witch."

"See if you can escape a noose witchy."

"Only one good witch, a dead one."

One of the men had a rope and was throwing it to the branches above while another man was climbing the tree ready to secure the rope.

"Oh no, this is not going to happen," Molly shouted in horror. "I'm coming Mary."

Mary's screams rent the air as she sobbed with pain and fear. "Let me go, I'm not a witch, I've done nothing wrong." Her pleading was landing on deaf ears.

Molly looked around for some way to free Mary. A squirrel chittered in the tree high above them. It held an acorn in its tiny paw. Seeing what the squirrel suggested she nodded, "yes do it." A whole family of squirrels appeared by its side and an avalanche of acorns fell hard from the tree hitting the men causing them to dive for cover away from the tree. The one climbing the tree slid quickly down as he tried to protect himself from the projectiles.

The ones holding Mary still held her though. Molly quickly picked up a stick, just two men left to deal with, she could do that. It had worked last time and this time she didn't hold back any punches. She hit them as hard as she could anywhere she could. Between the acorns and the stick, the men soon let go of Mary and headed for safety.

"Now Mary, run," Molly yelled.

Mary didn't need telling twice, she ran in the opposite direction from the men. She didn't stop to think about where she was headed, just getting away was all she could think about. Molly followed.

A badger emerged from its sett, chittering loudly. Molly thanked the badger and called out, "there are more that way Mary. Head towards the Hall, I have a plan."

Mary detoured again. Running in heavy seventeenth-century clothes wasn't easy. She had a stitch in her side, her head hurt where the men had pulled clumps of hair free, her face was red with the exertion and she couldn't get enough breath due to the stays in her bodice. Twigs and brambles pulled at her skirts slowing her down and wrestling holes in odd places.

A blackbird circled overhead singing loudly. "Follow the blackbird Mary."

"What?"

"Just do it. Trust me."

The sounds of tramping feet were drawing closer again as Mary stopped to take a breath and look for the blackbird. Spinning around she saw it on a low branch just above her. Running towards it, the blackbird took wing and slowly led Mary towards the edge of the woods. The sounds of footsteps receded.

On the blackbird flew, with Mary and Molly following. Molly wasn't out of breath at all, but poor Mary was really struggling now. Her legs were heavy as lead, her breath was coming in gasps and her heart beat so hard it felt like it was coming through her chest. "I have to stop," she said, bending forward as she tried to fill her lungs with air.

"Just a bit further Mary. Head to the bridge over the River Col."

The blackbird flew circles over Mary as it waited for her, encouraging her with its song. The sounds of people shouting and tumbling through the woods reached Molly's ears. "Come on Mary you have to move. They're coming."

Molly was edging out of the woods, calling constantly to Mary to move. A grassy field lay between the woods and the river. Colhome Hall could be seen in the distance. "Just a bit further Mary."

Taking a deep breath, Mary set off again. She had no idea what she would do when she got to the river, she hoped Molly had a good plan. The field was muddy, pulling on Mary's feet with a slurping sound with every step. Ankle boots protected her from the worst of the mud but the bottom of her skirts were shredded.

"Run towards the bridge Mary."

Glancing over her shoulder, Mary saw what looked like 20-30 men following her. She could see Mr Smith, but most of the men she didn't recognise. Where had they all come from? Seeing the men gave her a burst of speed. She didn't know how much longer she could run, she hoped she had enough energy left to get to the river.

As she approached the bridge she could see ducks swimming up and down, reeds in the water enough to pull a person under and fish by the dozen. Where was she supposed to go?

"Take your shoes off Mary and throw them to the side in the mud, anywhere, make it look like you dove in."

Still running towards the river Mary did as she was told, hopping on one foot as she removed each boot. Wool stockings protected her feet a bit, but sharp stones in the dirt made her grimace. Down the banking to the river she ran, throwing her boots sideways as she reached the water. One boot flew into a bush, the other on its side in the mud.

"You're going to have to wade in the water Mary, just enough so you leave no footprints. Head under the bridge. The banking sides are hiding you at the moment, but you need to be quick."

The bird sang its farewell as it flew off leaving Mary to follow Molly's instructions. Mud pulled at her feet as she waded towards the water, cautious of the reeds which would mean sure death. Water reached her waist, pulling at her long skirts making it hard to move, she pulled herself through with her hands cartwheeling in the air. Following Molly's instructions, she found herself under the bridge.

"I found this the other night, an otter showed it to me while you all slept. Feel along the bridge support wall Mary, there's a gap."

Mary did as she was told, the roughness of the wall pulled at her skin and nails. She bit her lip for silence as one nail wrenched loose. Then she felt it, the wall disappeared. Moving into the space that was black and invisible to the eye, she felt her way slowly. The gap widened as she got behind the bridge support.

Stopping, she stood in silence, slowing her breath so the gasps couldn't be heard, the quack of ducks and the lapping of water were the only sounds. She was shivering with the cold of the water and the fear in her heart. She slipped a finger between her teeth so the chattering couldn't be heard.

Then she heard the clamour of men running to the river

banking.

"Where'd the witch go?" asked one man.

"Looking like she might have jumped in," replied another.

"Aye her boots be here," said another.

"She couldn't survive those reeds, not um, not without the Devil's help." It was the man with the upside-down head.

Molly hadn't put herself behind the wall, she watched the men. Making sure they were convinced Mary was gone.

Mr Smith was one of the last to come alongside the river. Looking hot and sweaty, panting after his run, he took a moment before he said anything. "You sure she ain't hiding someplace?"

The men looked up and down the river, none of them very keen to get their feet wet by going in and checking under the bridge. One man, younger than the rest went onto the bridge, lay down and looked underneath. "Nothing here, no sign at all."

Molly was about to give a sigh of relief when she spotted Lawrence with James still hand-tied and gagged by his side.

"Footsteps lead to the river, only one way she could have gone." He didn't look sad, he looked elated, his face beaming. Totally focused on the river he didn't notice when James moved his hands to remove the gag.

James looked terrified with fear for Mary. "Mary," he yelled. "Mary-mol, where are you?" Then as realisation took him, he crumpled to the floor, "no, oh God, no."

Lawrence wasn't done though. "Check the bushes, bash the reeds. Make sure she isn't hiding. We stay here until nightfall, just to be sure."

The men started moving up and down the river, checking everywhere. Molly knew that Mary couldn't stand in the water until after nightfall, she would freeze to death. They would have to follow the space behind the wall and find out where it went.

"Move as quietly as you can Mary, hopefully, this gap leads somewhere."

In the darkness, Mary could only move forward by feeling the wall on both sides and tracking where it led. Molly followed.

Mary and Molly felt themselves moving upwards, out of the water, but in the pitch blackness, they had no idea which direction they were headed. All they could do was keep moving until eventually, they reached dry land. They were in a tunnel. With hands touching dirt on both sides of them, they inched forward, feeling the floor in front with their toes before setting a foot down. It was slow going. Mary's nose hit a wall before her toe found it. They had come to a dead end.

"There's nowhere to go Molly," Mary sobbed.

"There has to be, it can't be a dead end, what would be the point of a tunnel going nowhere?"

Mary sank to the ground.

Molly knew Mary was tired, her head hurt from ripped-out hair, her finger hurt where she tore the nail, her feet hurt from all the stones she had walked over and her skirt was sopping wet and stuck to her. On top of that, her boots were gone and she didn't possess another pair. How she wasn't crying Molly didn't know, but maybe she didn't have any tears left. She couldn't let her give up, she had to get out of this tunnel.

"Come on Mary, if you want to live we have to find a way

out of this tunnel, and get you home to safety. Your Mother will know what to do." Molly sounded positive, but inside she quaked. She had to get Mary to safety or she herself may never get home again.

Molly heard rather than saw Mary levering herself up, and feeling again at the walls, running her hands across the ones at the side of her and then the one in front. Molly copied her and then almost fell over as the wall disappeared. "Mary I found a gap," she said.

Molly had been wondering if she had taken Mary from the frying pan into the fire and if she could, she would have hugged Mary at that moment. "Come on, let's move. I don't like this tunnel any more than you do."

Molly felt again for the gap and carefully made her way through it. It was the same as the one near the river, a space that she had to sneak through and then around a corner. Once round the corner, Molly found herself in bright candlelight. She was in one of the alcoves off the tunnel that led between the cottage and the Hall.

"Wait here Mary, while I check the coast is clear."

Molly checked the tunnel, there was no one around. "Come on."

They found energy then to run, safety was so close. Down the tunnel they went and into the cellar of the cottage. At the pantry door they stopped and listened, they needed to be sure there was only family inside. They could hear Mother and Lizzie talking, but no one else. Cautiously Molly opened the door and peeked in.

"All clear Mary, up you go."

The fire was blazing, Mother was preparing dinner, and Lizzie was playing with wooden blocks with Alex. At Mary's bedraggled appearance they stopped and stared.

Mother was the first to find her voice. "What on Earth happened to you? Where's James? He promised to look after you. And where are your shoes?"

Hearing her Mother was the undoing of Mary, she ran to her and sobbed in her arms. Through hiccups of tears, she managed to tell her Mother what happened. How Molly had helped her and the secret tunnel. When she started to say James had betrayed her, Molly stopped her.

"No, he didn't Mary. He was bound and gagged, with a knife held to his ribs so he couldn't warn or help you. His brother started it. It was all Lawrence. I think he waited until he knew you were out with James and then gathered his undesirable men and set them after you."

"Truly? It wasn't James?"

"No Mary. In fact, I think he's heartbroken thinking you're dead at the moment."

Mary relayed what Molly had said, a small smile on her lips and hope in her eyes knowing James was still her friend.

Mother took charge and Molly was happy to let her. It was comforting to leave things to the adult.

"Be all this as it may, we're going to have to hide you. If Lawrence finds out you are still alive we'll have all this to go through again," Mother said. "Lizzie, you and I are going to have to put on a show to beat all shows. We have to pretend we believe Mary is dead. Can you do that?"

Lizzie looked at Mary. At the fear and pain written on her face. "Yes, I can do that. It breaks my heart to see her as she is, bleeding, wet, muddy and bootless. I just need to think of this and I can be upset. Don't worry Mary, they won't find you."

"Run upstairs quickly and find her some clean clothes. Come Mary, into the bolt hole. Hide down there, Lizzie can bring you some things. Take a hooded candle with you. I'll get this mud cleaned away."

Molly went into the hole with her. She couldn't leave Mary alone down there. She guessed Mary would be very frightened still.

The bolt hole proved spacious. A low roof meant Mary and Molly couldn't move around much, but Mary was safe and it was warm under the floor. Lizzie soon appeared with clean clothing, food and water. The door was closed and the cabinet replaced.

Sounds from the cottage drifted down. They remained quiet for a while, but nothing was happening other than the usual everyday things. Molly knew she needed to distract Mary and give her something to think about other than Lawrence and the awful events of today. Eventually, Molly asked, "What war is going on Mary?"

In the candlelight, Molly could see Mary's look of surprise. "The civil war of course. You know Roundheads and Cavaliers. King Charles against Parliament. You don't know about that?"

"Yes, I know of it, but I was never very good at history. There have been a few wars over the years and I couldn't remember which one would be now," Molly replied.

Mary gave Molly a history lesson while they shared the food that Lizzie had brought. "King Charles, he ruled everyone, made the laws and such, as has happened since forever. The King of the land always made the rules, but Parliament decided he was getting a bit too powerful and the people needed to have their say. He did stop Parliament from meeting for 11 years apparently. Mother says he is power-hungry. One minute she's backing him the next she hopes he falls. For myself, I don't know which is best. I will hide from them all.

The battles go on everywhere, but we have been lucky and the fighting is not close to us, Marston Moor was the closest big battle. Many men volunteered to fight, but some like my Father are needed for other skills. He's a carpenter so his skills are needed for building and repairing. I'm glad he doesn't go and fight, it must be awful. James's brother Caleb is with the King's army and his Father too.

The King had his Seat in York, but that was taken from him last year and is now run by Lord Fairfax. Father says he's a fair and just man. The King is not doing so well at the moment, Mother says it looks like he could lose. We keep this hidey-hole in case of danger. The tunnel is an escape for the Marquis and his family if they need it. I couldn't imagine running their way now for help. They likely would hand us over to whoever was most dangerous."

Molly pondered the information for a moment before asking, "why were those men that chased you not fighting the war?"

Mary sat quiet, chewing her food and didn't answer straight away. Molly waited, watching as Mary's eyes glistened with unshed tears. With a shake of her head, Mary blinked them away and with as steady a voice as she could muster she replied, "Mr Smith is an alcoholic and a wastrel. He wouldn't be fit to fight and I am guessing the other men have some other reason for not fighting. Some may be press-gang men. Impressment is used to recruit for the army, so they could be here for that. I am guessing Lawrence found them."

They had just finished eating when the sound of knocking could be heard. They both went silent.

Voices were muffled, they couldn't hear exactly what was said, but they did hear when Lizzie became hysterical and Mother screamed. Even Alex started bawling. Mary bit her lip. Molly could understand her worry. She knew they were pretending, but it sounded so real. She wanted to stop it, she couldn't bear the pain she could hear in their shouts. Moving towards the door of the bolt hole she was just about to unlatch it when Molly stopped her.

"Don't be stupid Mary. Remember they are pretending. They know you're fine. Just wait."

Mary sat down in the dirt again. "Sorry," she whispered. After a moment's thought she added, "thank you for being here Molly. I don't know what I would have done without you."

The waiting seemed to go on forever, but eventually they heard Mother shout, "get out. Get out of my house and never come back."

Footsteps sounded on the floor and the door banged shut

behind whoever had brought the news of Mary.

Another five minutes passed before they heard furniture moving above them and a knock on the trap door. Mary unbolted it and Mother helped her out. The curtains were closed and all the doors locked. It wouldn't seem strange to any passer-by as everyone thought they were in mourning. They were expected to do that.

"It was Lawrence," said Mother. "He tried to tell me that you were playing chase with his brother and slipped in the river. He brought your boots. I told him he was lying through his high-born teeth, you don't take boots off when you are running and playing games." She grinned then. "The look on his face was a picture. Anyway, he won't be back."

Mary flopped into the chair by the fire. "What are we to do though Mother? I can't stay hidden in here for the rest of my life."

"I thought of that. You can go to your Father. He's staying with cousin Sarah in York. We'll call you Molly in any letters or such like, in honour of our wonderful grandaughter and also because Mary-mol was a shortened Mary-Molly. From now on you will be known as Molly."

"The King lost York though, will it be safe?" Mary asked.

"Your father said in his last letter that it was business as usual there. You should be fine. Father can come for you, I will write to him. No one will think it strange that a Father comes home when his child has died. We can do this Mary. Everything will work out, you wait and see," Mother replied, then with a glance at Lizzie she looked thoughtful. "I'm sorry Lizzie, but we will have to postpone your wedding. It wouldn't be seemly to be married so soon after your sister's 'death'."

Lizzie shrugged her shoulders, "don't worry about that now, we can work out another date. We can sort it out later, Mary is the important one now. We have to see her safe."

Mary rose from the chair needing to hug her Mother again and Molly gratefully sank into it. She suddenly felt very tired. Not surprising really she thought, I haven't slept for almost 3 days. Looking at the family clamouring around Mary and making plans to keep her safe, she felt peaceful and relaxed. She knew it would be alright. Her eyes refused to remain open, she would close them for just a moment.

Chapter 14

When she woke up she felt much better. Stretching out she felt the softness of her bed. Then her eyes shot open, she was in her own bed. How? Was it a dream? Did it not really happen?

Throwing back the covers, she tumbled out of bed and looked down, she was fully dressed in the same jeans and t-shirt she had on when it all started. She smelled awful and her clothes were filthy and disgusting. The torch was still in her pocket, the knife tucked in her sock. Her trainers, muddy and wet, were still on her feet.

Falling back to sit on the bed she sat in stunned silence. It was real, all of it had really happened. How was she going to explain her state to Gran? The bedding would definitely need changing, Gran was going to be ten shades of purple when she saw the state of the bed. She would probably be grounded for the rest of the summer. She looked at the clock on the wall, 4 pm. This was all going to take some explaining, she needed a story, but she couldn't for the life of her think how to explain 3 missing days.

She was just checking her phone and finding that Aisha hadn't called when Ghost Mary appeared. A smiling happy Mary.

Thank you Molly. Good-bye.

Mary faded and in her place Molly caught a vision of Mary

and James walking hand in hand. They were surrounded by mud huts and the tallest trees Molly had ever seen. They were definitely not in England.

Molly knew she had to find Gran and at least let her know she was safe, even if she didn't know how she was going to explain her absence. Running from her room, Molly raced through the cottage calling "Gran, Gran, where are you?"

Downstairs there was no sign of Gran. Through the window, Molly could see a police car and fire engine parked outside. The pantry door was open and the light coming up from the cellar was very bright. Molly headed that way.

As she entered the cellar she realised the tunnel had caved in. Gran must think she was buried. There was a lot of noise, people and huge lights everywhere. Looking around she found Gran sitting on a chair someone must have brought down for her. She looked so old and small, sat there alone, wringing her hands in anguish. She was totally focused on the tunnel. Her eyes never moved from the men digging painfully slow making sure they wouldn't hurt Molly if they found her under the rubble. Molly's heart went out to her. Dashing down the steps she ran to Gran and putting her arm around her said, "it's ok Gran, I'm safe. I'm here.

Gran had been concentrating so hard on the work being done in the tunnel that she hadn't noticed Molly until she spoke.

"Molly, oh Molly. I was so frightened. Is it really you? Are you alright? Let me look at you." Gran took an arm's length look and then grabbed Molly in the biggest hug imaginable. The hug was soon over and Gran's fear turned to temper, even as the tears of joy ran down her face.

"Where the Hell have you been? Do you see the trouble you caused? And look at the state of you." Then the temper was gone and the joy of seeing Molly again took over. "Oh Molly, what happened? I was so worried."

All the workers stopped and stared. A policeman approached them. "So this is the missing Molly. Your Gran's been beside herself. How did you get out? Where did you come from?"

Wanting thinking time, Molly looked around at the mess. Dirt was everywhere, dug out and put in piles. A machine for digging stood idle, while shovels and rakes were in numerous hands. "I'll explain upstairs if that's ok, I don't particularly want to look at the tunnel again right now."

Gran and the policeman nodded and with Gran leading the way, and the policeman behind Molly, they headed to the living area of the cottage.

"You stink Molly, a quick explanation of where you have been for the last 2 hours and how you got out of the tunnel and then a shower for you," Gran said.

Molly thought quickly, she'd only been gone for 2 hours. 2 hours was much easier to explain than 3 days. She didn't look at either of them as she claimed to have been near the edge of the tunnel cave-in.

"I clambered out of the soil that fell from the tunnel walls and followed the tunnel to the Hall, then I walked back across the fields. I'm really sorry to have worried you all."

The policeman seemed satisfied but thoughtful, "So the tunnel leads up to the Hall, now there's a thing. Probably very old. You're a very lucky young lady," he said to Molly. Then addressing Gran he continued, "We'll leave you to it. You'll need to get someone in to make the tunnel safe though. I wouldn't advise going down there again until it's done." He headed back to the cellar muttering to himself and shaking his head, "would you believe it, the old Hall eh?

"Shower for you Molly, then we will talk some more," Gran said, before following the policeman back towards the cellar where everyone was gathering things together so they could leave.

Molly couldn't agree more. She really needed a shower and she was hungry, but shower first. She heard Gran thanking everyone in the cellar as she headed upstairs to the bathroom. Taking time away from everyone would give her a chance to remember her story. She needed to recite it backwards and forwards a few times so she didn't forget it. Try to make it real.

Everyone had left when she got back downstairs in clean clothes and smelling much nicer, wet hair dampening the back of her t-shirt. Gran was on the sofa twirling her thumbs as she waited. Molly headed straight for the fridge. "I'm hungry Gran, what can I have?"

"I'll make you a ham sandwich and you can start explaining. The policeman might have believed you, but the Hall is locked up today so how did you get out? And why are your trainers and jeans wet as well as muddy? You do know that most liars don't look anyone in the eye while they lie, you were looking at the floor. So out with it, there are too many holes in your story young lady. I want the truth."

Molly looked Gran in the eye and felt the heat rise up her neck into her cheeks as she realised she'd been caught in the lie. No matter how many ways she remembered the story, it was no good if Gran knew she was lying.

Taking a gulping breath she shook her head, "I don't think you'll believe me."

"Try me," Gran said.

Molly started slowly, explaining about Ghost Mary. When Gran said nothing, she continued gathering her courage from the excitement of knowing she had made a difference and the happy ending she had seen in her vision.

Between mouthfuls of ham sandwich and sips of hot chocolate, she told Gran how she had travelled through time and met their great, great and so many more greats Grandmother. Gran sat on the sofa, drinking tea and just listening until Molly came to the part about skills in the family.

Molly looked at Gran for confirmation.

Gran smiled, "yes, it's true. So you figured out that I can heal, but mine is a minor skill compared to yours I think. It seems to me, that you have visions of the past and can travel through time. Both are dangerous though, you must be very careful Molly."

"Yes, I know. Mary's mother told me about the Oracle thing. Is that what happened to Mum?"

Gran didn't say anything, she seemed to be considering what to say, but after everything Molly had been through she decided it was time for some truths of her own.

"Yes, your Mum sees visions all the time. Mostly they don't mean anything to her, but the one where your Dad had his accident, well she tried to stop it. The problem with visions is, that you can't stop them. This is what will happen or in your case, what did happen.

After you left for school, she thought we would all be better off without her, if you understand my meaning. I was so frightened for her, I had to call a doctor. They took her away, to a mental health hospital, but you were too young to understand. What was I supposed to say to you? You had lost your Father and your Mother was gone. I thought by saying 'grown-up stuff' you would stop asking questions." Gran smiled at Molly, "you never did. She's much better now, she can control the visions mostly with medication and we hope she can come home soon. She misses you very much."

Molly thought about it, she'd had visions and thought she was going crazy. At long last, she really understood what her Mum had been going through. Why she had left so quickly and in a strange way she found it reassuring.

"Oh I have another skill, at least I have it in the past, I don't know about now. I could understand animals and they understood me. They helped me save Mary."

Molly continued her story finishing with the vision just before she came downstairs.

Gran sighed and leaned back on the sofa, the look on her face one of admiration. "That is truly an amazing story. We should check the notebook, see if it's changed." Gran went to the drawer and withdrew the notebook and pocket watch. Turning over the watch she looked at the inscription.

Molly

My Love, My Life.

Neither Gran nor Molly said anything, they just looked, and then the hugest grin spread across their faces.

Gran passed the notebook to Molly. She opened it near the end. She would read it all later, but for now, she wanted to know what happened after she left.

As she flicked through, Gran stopped her, "what's that?"

A big grin lit Molly's face, "that," she said, "is the recipe for the cake. I asked Mary to put it in the notebook. She remembered."

Molly continued to flick through, "Gran look at this."

20th September 1654

James came to see me in York. This is to be the last of his visits for a long time. He is going to Africa. I thought my heart would break, but then he asked me to go with him. As his wife.

Thank you Molly. I am leaving this book where I know you can find it before I go. I thought you would like to know what happened.

Much love, Mary-mol.

Gran and Molly sat in silence. Gran gazed constantly at Molly. A little girl that had done so much. But, Molly wasn't a little girl anymore. Molly had grown up in the most wonderful of ways.

"I have a couple of questions though Gran, some things that puzzled me."

Gran waited.

"All the women in the family are called something Barber, I am Molly Barber. Even married women keep their maiden name. Why?" Molly asked.

"Ah, that is a very old story, which I would have told you eventually. It is older than your Mary-mol, so when she married James and changed her name, she knew what she was doing," Gran said.

"What do you mean?" asked Molly

"The story goes that one young Barber had 'witch sight', which is similar to what you can do, lots of different skills. Anyway, she met a handsome young man who swept her off her feet. They were married against the wishes of his family, they said she was not worthy of their name. Even so, she took his name as women are want to do when they love someone. As soon as she used her new name, all her powers were gone. Never again could she see Ghosts, help ill folk, see auras, nothing. Her man died young and after pressure from his family, she reverted to her maiden name. Her powers returned as soon as her name was changed. Now no Barber will ever change their name." Gran looked at Molly to make sure she understood.

Molly nodded thoughtfully then looking at Gran with hope in her eyes she asked, "why doesn't Mum just change her name then?"

"She didn't want to have a different name to you. It's that simple," Gran replied.

Molly stored that information away, she would talk to her Mum about it when she eventually got to see her again.

"So what is your second question?" Gran asked.

"Ghost Mary told me that they took her while her mother was at the Hall, and Lizzie and Alex were out in the woods, but that didn't happen at all. How come?" It was something that had puzzled Molly since the men had taken Mary. She hoped Gran had an explanation.

Gran smiled, "that's easy. You were there. You changed everything that people did, just by being there."

At Molly's puzzled look Gran tried again to explain.

"Think of it like this. If you were going to go out and someone knocked on the door, you wouldn't go when you planned to. You might not even go at all, depending on where you were going. You knocked on the door and they didn't go out. Sometimes you'll hear it called, 'flap of a butterflies wings,' which means, the smallest thing can change everything."

Molly looked thoughtful for a moment, then with a small smile said, "Thanks Gran."

***

Dashing upstairs Molly found her phone prostrate on the bed in her room. The battery was half full so she should have enough to call Aisha. She needed to tell her she could stop her searches and enjoy time with her Nan now. Ghost Mary was happy and if they looked deeply enough it was even possible that Aisha was related to Molly. She had a definite look of James about her.

Aisha answered instantly. "Hi Molly, I was just about to call you."

"Hi Aisha, you'll never ..." Molly started to talk, but Aisha interrupted.

"Nan is confused, the family tree changed and she can't understand why. So I need to tell you different stuff. Like the most amazing thing, somehow I am related to James. How awesome is that?"

Molly grinned, she had been right. She tried to butt in, but it was as if Aisha had been kept shut up for days and needed to talk. There would be no interrupting until she'd finished.

"Oh and another thing, you know I said about the lost fortune, well it was Caleb who lost it, James's brother. And his other brother, you'll never believe it but he died on his first day in Court. Someone tried to poison the King and Lawrence had the food instead or at least that's the story. Doesn't sound like a nice way to die, but there you go. James went to Africa and married someone called Molly too. There seem to be a lot of Molly's around. That's what has Nan most puzzled. She saw that James didn't marry and then he did and had children, quite a few apparently. All the notes and papers Nan collected have all changed. It's most odd."

At this point, Molly couldn't stop herself from laughing aloud. Aisha had barely paused for breath and answered all the things Molly wanted to know.

"What's so funny?" Aisha said. "I don't think being

poisoned is funny, or James marrying a Molly. Strange but not funny."

"Aisha, Molly is Mary. I have so much to tell you, but most can wait until you get back. Just so you know, you can relax, Ghost Mary is gone and she changed her name to Molly. Can't say I'm sorry about Lawrence either, but honestly this lot can wait. I just wanted to tell you to enjoy your stay in Scotland and I'll explain everything when you get back."

"You got rid of Ghost Mary? She's Molly? Explain yourself girl, I'm going nowhere until you give me all the details. And I do mean all!" Aisha was adamant.

"I don't have time right now Aisha," Molly tried to sound apologetic. There's just too much to tell. I'll reveal it all later, I promise. Now go and enjoy yourself with your Nan. I need to spend some time with Gran we have things to discuss."

"Ok, if you insist. But damn I wish I knew what was going on. Don't keep me waiting too long the suspense is killing me."

Molly laughed again. "I won't. Chat later. Bye."

Molly left the phone on her bedside table and headed downstairs. As Ghost Mary had said, she should appreciate her Gran. Not everyone had one.

Afterward

Recipe for Mary's Mothers Cake recipe:-

Take 6 quarts of fine flour well dried, 6 pounds of Currants, 2 pound of Butter, 3ʳˢ of a pound: of Beaten Almonds, 1 lb of Loaf Sugar. Nutmeg, Mace, Cinnamon, ginger enough to season it, a little salt put in the Butter in bits. Work it well with flour. Mingle the spices, sugar and almonds well together being beaten with Rosewater and sugar. Put in 4 quarts of good Ale yeast let it stand to rise awhile then have a posset ready of a quart of Cream and so much sack as to turn it tender, put in as much of the posset as will make the paste tender then let it stand to Rise before the fire close covered half an hour and work in yᵒᵘʳ fruit to which you may ad[d] a pound of raisons, stoned and cut in half a pound of sliced Dates. One hour and half will Bake it.

Many thanks to:

Joyce White for the authentic cake recipe, atasteofhistorywithjoycewhite.blogspot.com taken from Receipts Medicinal 17th c. Manuscript of John Evelyn of Surrey, England. Edited by Christopher Driver (1997)

About the Author

Diane Chesterton lives in the foothills of the Pennines in England with her husband and two Border Collies. A retired midwife, she has two children and four grandchildren.

Besides writing stories, she likes to walk the dogs, make beautiful cross-stitch pictures and play online games.